D1525780

FALSE JUSTICE

A JESSIE BLACK LEGAL THRILLER

LARRY A. WINTERS

Grave Testimony, the exciting prequel to the bestselling Jessie Black Legal Thriller series, is FREE for a limited time. Click here to tell me where to send your FREE copy of Grave Testimony:

http://larryawinters.com/read-gt

You will also be included in my free email newsletter, where you'll learn more about me, my writing process, new releases, and special promotions. I promise not to spam you, and you can unsubscribe at any time.

—Larry A. Winters

1

As a prosecutor, Jessie Black usually viewed defense attorneys as the enemy, but today, looking across the courtroom at Randal Barnes, she couldn't help feeling a pang of sympathy. The lawyer was leaning over sideways from his seat at the defense table, rummaging through an overstuffed attaché case, apparently searching for the right file amid of mess of other ones. His suit was wrinkled, his tie half-undone, and his hair stuck up in random clumps. His eyes were puffy and bloodshot.

The judge cleared his throat. "Mr. Barnes?"

"Sorry, Your Honor!" Barnes shot to his feet, knocking over his attaché case and spilling papers onto the floor. "I'm trying to find my notes."

Beside him at the defense table, Barnes's client, an overweight Latino man named Tomas Alvarez, closed his eyes and silently mouthed words. Maybe a prayer, Jessie thought. More likely a curse.

"You're the one who requested this hearing," the judge said.

Barnes's ears turned red. "Yes, Your Honor. And I'm prepared, but—"

"Apparently not. Let me refresh your memory." The judge

looked down at his own papers. "You submitted a motion seeking a one-month continuance on the basis that you need additional time to prepare for trial due to other cases preventing you from devoting the necessary time."

"Yes, Your Honor. That's correct." Barnes made a fumbling attempt to straighten his tie, then dropped his hands to his sides. "It's just bad timing, Judge," he went on in a weakened voice. "I've got a bunch of trials hitting at the same time. I'm stretched too thin."

The judge waved his hand dismissively. "Ms. Black, does the Commonwealth oppose?"

Jessie had spent the past four weeks gearing up for Alvarez's trial. Her opening statement was memorized. Her witnesses were ready to testify. And the victim's family was ready to endure the trial and hopefully find closure in a guilty verdict. But motions for continuance were commonplace, and, in this case, Barnes's seemed justified. Tomas Alvarez might be a murderer—Jessie was certain he was—but he was still entitled to a vigorous defense.

"No, Your Honor," she said.

The judge nodded. "The defense's motion is granted. Trial will be postponed one month. Mr. Barnes, I expect you will manage your calendar accordingly so that there are no further delays."

"Absolutely, Your Honor. Thank you." Barnes let out a long breath. Alvarez just shook his head, looking disgusted.

"The defendant will return to custody at the Curran-Fromhold Correctional Facility to await trial," the judge said. He banged his gavel and dismissed them.

Jessie gathered her files and headed out of the courtroom. With the Alvarez trial postponed, she had some unexpected free time on her hands. She'd have to talk to Leary. Maybe they could pull off a last-minute vacation together. The elevator doors opened and she stepped inside. She touched the button for the lobby.

"Hold that?"

She looked up and saw Barnes running toward the elevator. She kept the doors open for him. He stopped at her side, breathing heavily. *Maybe I'm not the one who needs a vacation.*

"You okay, Randal?" The elevator doors slid closed and they descended.

"Me?" He looked surprised by the question. "I'm great." He smiled at his own reflection in the metal elevator doors and tugged the lapels of his suit jacket. "Thanks, by the way. You really helped me in there."

"I know what it's like working hard on too many cases at once."

Barnes laughed. "Working hard or hardly working?" When she didn't join in his laughter, he looked at her quizzically. "You know that stuff about my workload was bullshit, right? I used it because I knew old Judge Bobblehead in there wouldn't risk violating Alvarez's Sixth Amendment right to counsel." He smoothed his hair into place and fixed his tie.

Had he played her? Jessie tried to think of a meaningful advantage Barnes might gain through a one-month continuance of the trial, but nothing significant came to mind. "If you're not really overloaded, why ask for a continuance?"

"Bills, Jessie." He rubbed his thumb and forefinger together. "Alvarez is my client, but the checks come from his mama. They're *supposed* to come, anyway. She's late. You know the best way to get a mother to pay? You throw her beloved baby boy's fat ass back in jail for a month, and let her know you won't hesitate to do it again."

"You asked for a continuance so you could extort his mother?" Jessie felt a tightness in her chest.

"He's been crying to her every chance he gets. About how the guards beat him. The other inmates beat him. His cell mate hit him so hard he spent a night in the infirmary."

"And instead of trying to help, you extend his suffering?"

"She'll pay up now. With interest."

Jessie shook her head and turned away from him.

"Don't act all indignant," he said. "I do the work. I'm entitled to my fee."

"It's unethical."

"He's a scumbag."

"He's your client."

"According to you, he's a murderer. You want to put him in prison for life, right? What does one more month matter?"

"For one thing, he hasn't been found guilty yet. Is this a trick your old boss taught you?" She knew Barnes used to work for Noah Snyder, a Philly-area lawyer not known for his ethical exactness.

"Learn from the best."

"Noah Snyder is not the best. He's not the lawyer you want to emulate."

"I've been doing pretty well for myself so far."

The elevator doors opened. Barnes stepped forward, but Jessie caught his arm. "What you did today was wrong, Randal. You have a duty to advocate for your client. Acting against his interests to put pressure on his mother so you can get paid.... I don't know what Noah Snyder taught you, but that's not how the legal system works."

Barnes looked at her with an expression that seemed to teeter between amusement and disappointment. "Jessie, that's exactly how the legal system works."

Barnes strolled out of the elevator. "I have a meeting with a certain mother and her checkbook. See you in a month."

2

JESSIE WATCHED Barnes weave his way through the courthouse lobby. The Criminal Justice Center was crowded as usual, and she lost sight of him within seconds. Sighing, she stepped out of the elevator and into the noisy chaos.

The sick feeling in her stomach had not dissipated, and she was surprised by its visceral intensity. His attitude had affected her more strongly than she could explain. When she'd woken this morning, she'd known Barnes's motion to postpone the Alvarez trial would probably be granted, but she'd felt happy and optimistic anyway. Now, after an elevator conversation that could not have been more than a minute long, she seemed filled with a dark feeling of gloom.

Shake it off, Jessie.

So Barnes had misused the system. Why should that bother her to this extent? There were always lawyers who behaved unethically. Despite what Barnes might believe, most did not. Barnes was the minority. Overall, justice prevailed. She'd seen it firsthand throughout her career.

"Jessie?"

Lost in her thoughts, Jessie almost didn't notice a woman

wending her way through the crowd in her direction. Recognizing her, Jessie felt her melancholy vanish in an instant. She smiled. "Kelly?"

All thoughts of Randal Barnes fled from her mind, replaced with warm memories. She had not seen Kelly Lee in what—ten years? Probably not since the day they'd both graduated from Penn Law. Kelly hadn't changed at all. Same petite frame, long black hair, expressive eyes. It wasn't until Kelly reached her that Jessie realized she was not smiling back. She looked upset.

"Is something wrong?"

"I was hoping to find you here," Kelly said. "You're probably busy, but—"

"Actually, my trial just got postponed."

Kelly's gaze seemed to scan the crowded lobby, as if watching for someone. "Your office told me you were in court today, so I came here. I ... I don't know who else to talk to at this point."

"What's wrong?"

"Is there somewhere we can talk in private?"

"An attorney conference room?" Jessie said. Each courtroom had a small attorney conference room outside of it, for use by lawyers and witnesses, family members, clients, and others. When Kelly nodded, Jessie ushered her into the elevator and they went to the conference room outside the now-vacant courtroom where Barnes had been granted his continuance.

Jessie gestured at one of the metal chairs, then took a seat in the other one. The table between them was mottled with stains, its edges dulled by many nervous hands. The air had an unpleasant odor, as if the room had trapped someone's bad breath. But Kelly barely seemed to notice their surroundings.

"It's been so long, but I feel like we were in class together yesterday," Jessie said.

With a wistful smile, Kelly said, "You look great."

"You, too."

Kelly looked around. Her nose wrinkled as she finally seemed to take in their squalid surroundings. "Back when we were studying for our Contracts exam, I never would have imagined you working for the city as a homicide prosecutor."

"I didn't think you'd become a personal injury lawyer."

Jessie immediately regretted the comment. She knew Kelly's area of the law was considered shabby in many circles. People— even other lawyers (maybe *especially* other lawyers)—mocked personal injury lawyers with derogatory names. *Ambulance chasers. Bottom feeders.* But if Kelly was offended, she didn't show it.

"I wanted to run my own firm. I have an entrepreneurial spirit, I guess."

"That's really impressive. I don't think I could do that—strike out on my own like that."

"Don't sell yourself short." Kelly looked down at her hands, and Jessie noticed the woman's fingernails were ragged, chewed. "Remember how worried you were about our Contracts final? And you aced it."

"I do remember that."

"I doubt there's anything you couldn't do if you put your mind to it."

"Kelly, tell me what's going on."

Kelly seemed to hesitate. "I think someone wants to hurt me."

"Have you gone to the police?" Jessie felt a bolt of adrenaline.

"Yes. They told me there's nothing they can do. Not unless someone makes an overt threat, or actually tries to harm me. Just the feeling that I'm being followed around, that's not enough for them to act on, apparently. And besides that, you probably know about...." She looked away and her voice trailed off.

Jessie leaned forward. "I probably know about what?"

Kelly shook her head. "Nothing. I'm sure the police are just following protocol. They can't spend all their time and resources protecting every person who feels threatened. I understand that."

"Why do you feel threatened?" Jessie said.

"I'm working on something big. A case that could cost some rich people a lot of money. Maybe worse." She paused and seemed to study Jessie, as if deciding whether to trust her.

"You came to me, Kelly. If you don't tell me what's going on, how can I help you?"

Kelly took a deep breath. "About a month ago, a husband and wife came to my office. Parents. They'd just lost their two-year-old son. They were grief stricken, but also angry. One day he was a normal toddler, and the next he was struggling to breathe. They took him to their pediatrician, who diagnosed him with restrictive airway disorder—it's common, usually a minor condition for kids. The pediatrician prescribed an inhaler. But the same night after visiting the pediatrician, he suffocated in his sleep and died. Acute respiratory failure."

"That's awful."

"I hear a lot of awful stories in my line of work. I guess you do, too."

Jessie nodded.

"The parents wanted to hire me to pursue a med-mal claim against the pediatrician. They believed their son's death had been unnecessary, that the doctor caused it by failing to properly diagnose his condition. I agreed to look into the claim." She ran her fingertip along a rough line of graffiti someone had gouged in the table's surface. "The way I work usually is that I will consult with a trusted expert to see if a claim has validity. If it does, I will usually take a case on a contingency basis. If I win, I get a percentage of the damages or settlement awarded to my client. Usually one-third. If I lose, I bill nothing. That's my risk."

She looked up at Jessie. "The parents were okay with this and agreed to wait for me to look into the claim and get back to them. I know a doctor, an MD, PhD. Great expert witness. I brought him the information and the file on the case."

"What did you find?"

"Not what I expected."

"The pediatrician didn't screw up the diagnosis?"

"Oh, he did, but that was the least of it. My guy's findings suggested that the condition itself had been brought on by exposure to excessive levels of formaldehyde. He proposed examining the family's living area to try to identify the source. We found it. A toy called Dinowarrior—it was a popular gift for boys last Christmas. The toy tested extremely high for levels of formaldehyde. The parents confirmed that the toy had been their son's favorite gift and that he'd been inseparable from it. That toy killed him."

Jessie suppressed a shiver. "So the parents have a claim against the toy manufacturer?"

"Potentially huge," Kelly said. "We filed a complaint against the company and a motion to certify the case as a class action."

"How many of these toys were sold?"

"Thousands."

In her head, Jessie put the pieces of Kelly's story together. "Someone from the company threatened you?"

"Not exactly. But ... I don't know. It's like I'm being followed. Like someone is watching me. I feel like someone wants to do me harm."

"Kelly, you're not giving me much to work with here."

She hesitated. "I can tell you the toy company is Boffo Products Corporation. They're big, but they started as a local company. Their headquarters is still based right outside of Philly."

"And the name of the family who lost their son?"

Kelly hesitated again. "Rowland."

"I can understand this Boffo company fighting you in court, but to come after you personally? That seems unlikely, doesn't it?"

Kelly brought a hand to her face and gnawed on the nail of her index finger. She seemed to realize she was doing it and stopped, intertwining her fingers on the table instead. Jessie waited patiently.

"There's more to it," Kelly said.

"I'm listening."

"I have reason to believe the president of the company, a man named Douglas Shaw, knew about the risk, but continued to distribute the toys anyway. He intentionally put his company's profit above children's safety."

"You can prove that?"

"I'm not sure how much I should tell you, Jessie. I don't want to put you in danger, too."

"I'm an assistant district attorney. I'm not an easy target."

Kelly nodded and took a deep breath. "All I'll say is that someone within Shaw's company reached out to me, a person with a guilty conscience. This person told me that Shaw knew about the danger. This person assured me that the evidence is there. I guess we'll find out during discovery, but I believe this person."

Jessie absorbed the information. "If that's true, Shaw could face criminal charges."

"Exactly. No amount of insurance will protect him from that. So he does have a reason to come after me. Self-preservation."

Jessie watched the woman. She looked genuinely afraid.

"I hate to impose on you," Kelly went on, "and ask a favor like this, but you're the only person I know connected with law enforcement. Can you talk to some of your friends in the police department? Get them to help me? I don't need a full-time bodyguard or anything, just someone to look into this, see if I'm being targeted. I'm thinking any police involvement at all might be enough to scare off Shaw."

"Of course," Jessie said. "I'll make a call. Why wouldn't I?"

Kelly shifted her gaze away, and for a second Jessie thought she might actually answer the rhetorical question. "Look, I didn't go into public service like you. Most of what I do—it's like a game. Someone will come to me claiming an injury. Half the time, it's made up or exaggerated. But if I think I can sell it in court, I'll take the case." She seemed to watch Jessie's reaction closely, and although Jessie struggled to hide her distaste, it must have shown. "I know that sounds bad, but the insurance companies are even worse. They'll happily collect their premiums, but the moment someone makes a claim, they'll use any excuse to avoid paying on a policy. My job is to negotiate with them—sometimes even begin a trial—and eventually there's a settlement payment. It's how the system works."

Jessie thought of her elevator chat with Randal Barnes. He'd said something similar, and similarly unconvincing to Jessie.

"But the Rowlands' case is different," Kelly said. "Do you understand? The Rowland case is a chance for me to actually do something good. I know that sounds stupid. Naïve."

"Not to me," Jessie said.

Kelly nodded. "You'll help me?"

"I'll help you."

THE WALK from the Criminal Justice Center to Police Headquarters took about fifteen minutes. Jessie spent most of that time in her own head, thinking about her conversations with Randal Barnes and Kelly Lee. By the time the distinctive, curving edifice of Police Headquarters loomed above her—the building was called the Roundhouse because of its shape—she barely remembered the walk.

She entered the Roundhouse and exchanged smiles and hellos with half a dozen cops before reaching the Homicide Division's bullpen. She found Detective Emily Graham sitting at a computer.

When she'd first met Graham a few years ago during a school shooting case, the two hadn't exactly hit it off. Graham seemed to think of the DA's Office as a necessary evil her job forced her to deal with, rather than as a partner. But while working together on that case, they'd discovered an unlikely friendship. Now, Jessie considered Graham her best friend, and was pretty sure the feeling was mutual.

Graham looked up, saw Jessie, and smiled. "What's up, Legal Eagle?"

Jessie leaned against the desk. "You sound uncharacteristically upbeat."

"What are you trying to say? You don't think I'm an upbeat person?"

"You're a very upbeat person."

"Yeah, well, I just closed a major murder case. So that helps."

"Congratulations."

"Another killer off the street. Assuming the lawyers don't screw everything up and render my months of dedicated work worthless."

Jessie knew better than to take the comment personally. "Now that's the cynical Emily Graham I know."

Graham laughed. "What's going on? Aren't you supposed to be in court for that Alvarez case?"

"The judge granted the defense a continuance."

Graham made a face. "You've been prepping for that trial for weeks. On the bright side, I guess you'll have some free time."

Jessie nodded. "I was thinking maybe a last-minute vacation, if Leary can get away. Did I tell you we're going out to dinner tonight with my dad? Since it's restaurant week, I made reservations at a nice French place."

"Good idea. Is that your dad's style, though?"

"I'm hoping he'll like it."

"Well, tell them both I said hi."

"I will." She paused. "Emily, I'm actually here to ask a favor."

Graham rolled her swivel chair away from her computer. "What's up?"

"There's a lawyer, a friend of mine from law school. She's involved in a case against a big company and she thinks someone might be following her."

Graham's eyes narrowed. "Did she go to the police?"

"She says they brushed her off."

"Really? That doesn't sound likely."

Jessie shrugged. "I agree, but that's what she says happened. I was hoping you could throw your homicide detective weight around, get someone to look into it."

Graham seemed to consider the request. "I am very powerful around here," she deadpanned.

"You're practically the commissioner."

"Okay, give me the details. What's this lawyer's name?"

"Kelly Lee."

Graham seemed to flinch at the name. She looked away. "I just remembered, I need to meet with the medical examiner."

"Now?"

"Yeah." Graham rose from her chair.

Jessie tried to make sense of the sudden change. "Are you okay?" She watched as Graham grabbed her suit jacket from the back of her chair and shrugged her arms into the sleeves.

"I lost track of time," Graham said. "Sorry. I need to run."

"Will you help with my friend?"

Graham continued to avoid eye contact. "I'll call you."

Graham started walking away from her desk. Jessie pursued her. They navigated between workspaces in the overcrowded bullpen. "Emily, look at me."

Graham stopped. "What?"

"Obviously I said something that upset you."

The detective looked like she might deny it. She seemed to study Jessie for a second, then let out a breath. "You know how I feel about lawyers."

"Me excluded." It was an old joke between them. Jessie said the words almost automatically.

"Kelly Lee isn't some heroic lawyer fighting for justice," Graham said. "She's a liar who will do anything to make a buck."

"You know her?" Jessie could not mask her surprise.

"Not personally. But I know she's brought a ton of police misconduct suits against the PPD. Did you know the city pays out nine-million dollars on average every year to settle claims against police officers? Do you know how much the city has to pay for reinsurance premiums alone because of all these claims?"

Graham's voice rose. The squad room was mostly deserted, thankfully, but the few cops in the room had turned to watch the confrontation. Jessie could feel the weight of their stares.

"I didn't know Kelly was involved in police misconduct litigation."

Graham tilted her head and offered a big, fake smile. "Well, now you know."

The intensity of Graham's response surprised her. Jessie could almost feel the heat of her friend's anger radiating from her body. "I didn't realize this was an issue so close to your heart."

"It should be close to your heart, too. These settlements come out of a tax-payer-funded city budget. And lawyers like Lee tarnish your profession."

"Maybe you're too close to this to be objective." Jessie regretted the words the moment they left her mouth.

"I'm completely objective."

"Don't you think the police should be held accountable if they abuse their authority?"

Graham rolled her eyes, a mannerism Jessie had found infuriating during her first interactions with the detective. "These cases aren't real, Jessie. They're cooked up by greedy lawyers."

Against her will, Jessie found herself remembering something Kelly had said to her. *Most of what I do—it's like a game.* She mentally shook off the voice in her head. "*All* of the claims? You can't believe that."

"Look, if Kelly Lee feels scared, she can use some of the money she took out of our pockets and hire a security guard. I'm not going to help her, and I doubt you'll find anyone in the department who feels differently."

Jessie watched, stunned, as Graham strode out of the Homicide Division, leaving her to wonder what the hell had just happened. And why the hell Kelly Lee hadn't warned her about her reputation with the PPD.

4

MR. AND MRS. MARK LEARY, he thought, savoring the words in his head.

"Leary, are you even listening?"

Mark Leary jumped. He had no idea where the conversation had gone, or even who had been speaking. He looked from Jessie to her father and felt his cheeks redden. "Sorry, I've got work on my mind."

Jessie's father shook his head. "The two of you, always thinking about work. It was your idea to take me to this *hoity-toity* place. You could at least be mentally present."

"*Hoity-toity*?" Jessie said, arching an eyebrow.

Her father shrugged. "You prefer *fancy-schmancy*?"

"How about elegant?"

Watching the two of them banter, Leary couldn't suppress a smile. It had occurred to him that Harland Black might not feel at home in a French restaurant full of well-dressed people sitting at tables covered in spotless white tablecloths, speaking in subdued voices against a background of classical music, clinking silverware, and decanting wine. But he'd kept the thought to himself because Jessie was excited about the idea. It was Restaurant Week in Philadelphia, and Jessie wanted to take her father out for a nice dinner. That was sweet, and he knew her father would appreciate the gesture even if he didn't appreciate the "*hoity-toity*" ambiance.

Even better, it dovetailed beautifully with Leary's own plans.

Under the table, he forced himself to stop tracing the circular shape in his pants pocket. "I'm mentally present now. What did I miss?"

"I was just telling Dad how great it is to work together, now that you're a detective at the DA's Office," Jessie said. "Walking to work in the morning, seeing you in the halls, that kind of thing."

"And you thought combining our work lives with our private lives would be a recipe for disaster," he reminded her.

"I did think that. But now that it's happened, I have to admit it's really nice."

"Better than nice. It's great."

"I was just kidding about the restaurant," her dad said. "The food looks pretty good. Even if I can't pronounce any of it."

"Next time," Leary said, "we'll let you pick the place."

"Deal."

"Excuse me," Jessie said, rising from her chair. "I'll be right back. I need to use the ladies' room."

Finally, Leary thought. He waited until Jessie disappeared through the doorway to the restrooms, then turned to her father. The man stared back at him and an awkward silence descended. Leary fought the urge to spout small talk about the Phillies or the Eagles. He didn't know how much time he would have before Jessie returned.

He cleared his throat and leaned forward, struggling to remember the words he'd thought up the night before. *It would mean so much to me to receive your permission.* No. *Your blessing.* No. *Your—*

"You watch the Eagles game last night?" Harland said.

Leary cringed inwardly, but nodded with what he hoped looked like enthusiasm. "Close game."

"Hell of a close game. If I had money on it, I think I might've had a heart attack. But I don't bet. You?"

"No, I'm not a big gambler." How the hell was he going to segue from gambling to asking this man if he could marry his daughter? He took a deep breath. "Mr. Black, there is actually something I wanted to talk to you about."

"Don't call me Mr. Black, Mark. I'm Harland."

"Okay, Harland. Anyway, I was hoping we'd have some time to talk because—"

Jessie's father looked up. Leary followed his gaze and saw Jessie returning to the table. She sat down, replaced her napkin on her lap, and smiled at both of them. "Did I miss anything?"

"We were just talking about the Eagles game," Harland said. "And Mark wanted to ask me about something."

Jessie looked interested. "Ask him about what?"

Leary tried not to squirm, but the evening was not going according to plan. When it came to romance, nothing ever seemed to go according to his plans. Sometimes he considered it a miracle he was in a relationship with Jessie at all. "Just sports stuff," he said lamely.

It looked like Jessie might push for a better explanation, but at that moment, the waiter arrived with their entrées. The plates were distributed on the table and the focus shifted to the beautifully presented dishes. Lamb for Leary, beef for Harland, and Mediterranean sea bass for Jessie. Jessie leaned over her plate and inhaled, smiling with anticipation. Leary picked up his knife and fork and made a show of busying himself, hoping the conversation would be dropped.

"This is so nice, having dinner with both of you," Jessie said. "Especially after the day I've had."

"Jessie's murder trial got postponed," Leary explained to Harland. "She spent the last month obsessively preparing for it."

She shot him a look. "I wasn't obsessed. I was diligent."

Her father nodded. He forked some food into his mouth, chewed, and swallowed. He smiled and said, "Good steak."

"And that's not why my day was hard. I got into an argument with Emily, and—" There was a buzzing sound and both Leary and Jessie reached for their phones. He saw Jessie's father smirk knowingly. Leary's phone was still, so it was Jessie receiving the call. She looked at her phone's screen and her face scrunched up in a way that Leary knew meant she was about to reluctantly excuse herself.

"Work?" Leary said.

"No. It's Emily." She glanced at her father, and Leary saw the indecision in her eyes. "It's okay. I'll call her back."

"No," Leary said. He couldn't let another chance to be alone with her father slip by. "You should talk to her."

"You sure?"

Both Leary and Harland nodded. "It's fine," Harland said. "Just don't let your food get cold."

"Thanks. I'll be quick."

Leary watched her walk away, then leaned toward Harland, not wanting to waste a second this time. "What I wanted to talk to you about is..." He hesitated. "I need to ask you.... Damn, this is awkward."

Jessie's father stared at him with an amused expression. "It's starting to be."

"You know Jessie and I have been together for almost five years."

"You make my daughter very happy."

"Thanks. It means a lot to hear you say that. The reason—"

Jessie returned before he could finish his sentence. The distraught look on her face drove all other thoughts from his mind. He jumped up and rushed to her side, almost knocking over his chair. "What's wrong?"

She looked into his eyes. Her gaze was watery, stricken. "I need to get to Walnut and 17th Street. Can you drive me there?"

"In the middle of dinner?" her father said. He had risen from his seat to join them. The three of them stood together in the middle of the dining room. Everyone seemed to be staring at them.

"I'll make it up to you, Dad. I promise."

Her father waved away her words. "If something's wrong, don't worry about me. Do what you need to do."

Jessie looked relieved. "Thanks, Dad."

"But I'm taking your food home with me. I'm eating well this week."

"It's a deal," Jessie said. She smiled, but Leary noticed her smile failed to reach her eyes. She tugged his arm, and they hurried out of the restaurant and into the night.

5

BURNT PLASTIC. Gasoline. Smoke. She smelled the accident before she saw it.

"You want to tell me what's going on?" Leary said. He pulled to the side of the road where a police barricade cut off access to the intersection of 17th and Walnut, the address Graham had given Jessie over the phone.

Jessie couldn't answer him yet. Feeling nausea rush up her throat as she climbed out of his car, she put her hand over her mouth.

Rescue workers milled around the remains of a Volkswagen Jetta. Smoke billowed from the misshapen husk. The car had apparently slammed into the brick wall of an apartment building—narrowly missing the glass entrance to a pizza place next door—colliding with enough force to crumple the vehicle like an accordion. The impact must have caused an explosion, because the car and the shattered wall were singed black. There were no flames now, but the remains of the car were charred and dripping with the water that had been used to douse the fire. The air stank.

Leary put an arm around her, but she gently pushed him away.

"I think I knew the person in that car," she said.

He looked at her, eyes wide. "Who?"

Emily Graham made her way through the police officers and rescue personnel to Jessie's side. Seeing her was a relief, despite the recent tension between them.

"Thanks for calling me," Jessie said.

"I thought you'd want to know."

Jessie tried not to shudder. "How many people were in the car?"

"Just the driver. Female. Like I said on the phone, the car is registered to Kelly Lee. We'll need a few hours to confirm that she was the driver."

"A few hours?" Leary said.

Graham turned to him. "The body isn't in good shape."

The body. Jessie swallowed. She had to struggle to voice the next question. "She died?"

Graham gazed at the wreck. "It's pretty bad, Jessie. We're talking body-parts-separated-from-the-body bad. And everything is severely burned. The ME is going to have to do some work."

Leary shook his head. "Jesus."

"What happened?" Jessie said. "Was there another car involved? Did the driver just lose control?"

"I don't think they're sure yet." Graham gestured at a group of men and women studying the wreck. "There weren't any witnesses—none who've come forward, anyway. No cameras on this intersection, either. We'll have to wait for AID's findings."

Jessie knew that AID stood for Accident Investigation Division, the Police Department agency tasked with investigating crashes in Philadelphia. She watched them work, feeling her skin crawl at the methodical way they examined the horrific scene. Leary made another attempt to put his arm around her shoulders. This time, she let him.

"Is AID aware of what Kelly told the police?" Jessie said. She struggled to keep her voice neutral, but saw Graham's expression tighten.

"I passed along the information." Her tone was cold.

"They know she thought she was being threatened?"

"I just told you I passed along the information."

Jessie nodded. "Okay. Thanks."

The detective shrugged. "I doubt they'll do anything with it."

"What?"

"I told you how the department feels about Kelly Lee."

Jessie wanted to be civil, but she couldn't contain her anger. "That can't matter now. A woman is dead. The police need to look into a company called Boffo Products Corporation, and its chief executive, a man named Douglas Shaw. Shaw may have targeted Kelly in order to shut down a lawsuit that would have hurt his company and exposed him to criminal charges. There's motive here. Suspicious circumstances."

Leary looked at Jessie. His eyes narrowed. "Why am I starting to get the feeling I'm not in the loop here?"

"That's up to AID," Graham said.

Jessie pulled her aside. "Emily, come on. You're a cop with integrity. I need you to help me here."

"Am I a cop with integrity?" Graham's face suddenly twisted with a look of disgust so visceral it made Jessie take a step back. "That's not what Kelly Lee claimed in the complaint she filed against me."

Jessie felt her mouth hang open. For a second, she had no words. "You never told me."

"Not something I'm super proud of."

"What happened?"

"What do you think? Lee and her scumbag client made up some lies about me. The city settled the case. We all signed nondisclosure agreements."

Jessie felt an ache in her chest. "I had no idea. I'm so sorry."

"Why?" Graham leaned forward, getting in Jessie's personal space. "Lawyers like Lee fulfill a vital function, right? Isn't that what you believe? To stop bad cops like me."

"It must have been a misunderstanding. Maybe Kelly was misled—her client lied to her."

"She's the liar. I got off lucky. God knows how many good cops' careers she ruined. And not just cops. She's sued doctors, firefighters, even other lawyers. This...." She gestured at the horrific accident scene. "A lot of people would call this karma."

"Would you?"

Graham turned away. Jessie could see her gnaw at her lip. "I don't believe in that stuff."

"I know. You believe in justice. Maybe Kelly was what you say—a liar—but if she was murdered, that's a heinous crime. We can't let a killer walk away just because the victim had flaws."

Graham shook her head. A rueful smile crossed her face. "Not my call. I told the investigators Lee thought someone was following her. What they do with that information is up to them. My conscience is clean."

"Jessie?" Leary said, joining them.

"I'll tell you everything later," she said to him. Then, turning back to Graham, she said, "Kelly was frightened for her life. Now she's dead. Don't you think that warrants a real investigation? Shouldn't the Homicide Division get involved?"

"This is AID's case until they find evidence to suspect a homicide."

"There must be something you can do."

Graham frowned and watched the AID investigators with a

melancholy expression. Someone made a joke, and several cops laughed. Graham's expression was like stone.

Leary looked at Jessie with concern. "We should probably go," he said. "Let the accident investigators do their job. Come on. I'll drive us home."

6

THE NEXT MORNING, Jessie tapped the doorframe of her boss's office and smiled at him when he looked up from his papers. "Got a minute?"

Warren Williams let out a sigh. His face creased with the beleaguered expression she'd gotten used to during her years working for him in the DA's Homicide Unit.

"Is this a bad time?" she said.

"No, come on in. I'm just wiped out. I've been waking up at 5:00 AM every morning for the past six days."

"Why 5:00 AM?" Jessie navigated carefully from his doorway to one of the visitor chairs in front of his desk. It was a short, but perilous, path, since there were documents piled on every available surface, including the floor. Her leg touched the edges of a tower of paper, and her breath caught in her throat, but the precarious stack didn't spill. She reached the chair with a small sigh of relief.

Warren didn't seem to notice. He was rubbing his eyes. "I heard on a podcast that most successful people rise early and meditate before work, so I'm trying it."

"You're meditating?"

He put his hands down and leaned back in his chair. "Well, no. For now, I'm just drinking coffee and trying to keep my eyes open. I'll start the meditation after I get used to waking up."

"Sounds like a plan." To her, it sounded like a crazy plan, but she didn't say that to Warren. She'd come to his office to ask for some time to look into Kelly Lee's death, not to critique his new morning ritual. "If it works for you, maybe I'll give it a try. Listen, the reason I'm here.... I need a favor, Warren."

Warren rocked back in his chair and his head entered a shaft of sunshine that filtered in through the room's only window. Instead of brightening his face, the crisp, fall sunlight seemed to accentuate the puffy evidence of fatigue.

"And what favor might that be?"

"You heard the Alvarez trial got postponed?"

Warren nodded.

"Well," she went on, "now I have some time on my hands, and I think I have a good use for it. A friend of mine from law school was in a car accident last night. She died."

Warren watched her. The look of sympathy she'd expected did not appear. "I'm sorry to hear that." His voice sounded strangely neutral and flat.

"The thing is, I'm not sure it was really an accident. Yesterday, she told me she felt threatened, like someone might be following her. I'd like to spend some time looking into it."

"Isn't that the PPD's job?"

"Yes, but...." She knew she needed to tread carefully. Throwing around accusations about the police shirking their responsibilities would not play well with Warren. "It never hurts to add a fresh perspective to the investigation, right? I'm a lawyer, so I have some insight into her daily routine. And I knew her. I think I can be helpful."

Jessie held her breath as Warren seemed to consider her request. "Does this law school friend's name happen to be Kelly Lee?"

Jessie tried to cover her surprise, but probably did a poor job of it. How did Warren always seem to know everything? It was like he had eyes and ears everywhere in the DA's Office and the Philadelphia Police Department. Everywhere in the city, it sometimes felt like. "I guess you already know that's her name."

He leaned forward. "I do know it. I also know that calling her your 'friend' is a bit of a stretch. My understanding is you haven't really spoken with her in about ten years or so. I also heard that the Accident Investigation Division found no evidence to suggest foul play. The formal report will be issued soon—probably today. There's not going to be any investigation for you to help with."

Jessie felt her face redden. "You've been looking into this."

"Of course I have. It's my job to manage this unit, including you."

She took a breath. "Well, if AID is not going to investigate, isn't that all the more reason I should take a look? With my trial delayed, I have time. AID might be right, but why not double-check? It will give me something to do, keep me busy, and I can feel like I'm helping Kelly, since I can't help her in any other way."

The smile that creased Warren's face was utterly devoid of mirth. "Being your boss brings me plenty of challenges. Keeping you busy isn't one of them."

"Is that a yes or a no?"

"I'm sure you've heard by now that Lee was not a popular figure within Philly law enforcement circles. Any 'double-check-ing' of the AID investigation is not going to be viewed as helpful. You're going to make enemies. And when *you* make enemies, *my* life gets harder. I can find you something to do if you're really so bored and directionless, believe me. That won't be a problem."

"Warren—"

"Let me be clear. Do not use the resources of this office to pursue any kind of investigation involving Kelly Lee."

7

JESSIE WAS on her second cup of coffee when Leary entered the coffee shop. She watched him scan the room. When he finally spotted her in the dark corner where she'd chosen a table, he smiled. It was almost enough to make her feel better.

"Not your usual coffee source," he said as he took the seat next to her. "Did Alish close his store today or something?" He was referring to the convenience store near the DA's Office where Jessie religiously purchased her morning coffee.

"Alish never closes his store."

He smiled again. "That I believe."

"I picked this café because we need to talk. That's hard to do in a convenience store—no matter how good the coffee is there."

"You do know we both work for the DA's Office now, right? Finding a place to talk isn't much of a challenge."

"We need to talk *privately*."

Leary looked intrigued. She sipped her coffee and watched him process her words. "This is about Kelly Lee's accident?" he said.

"Warren doesn't want me to get involved."

Leary pulled his chair closer to hers and touched her arm. "I'm sorry. I know you feel like you need to do something."

"No one else is."

Leary made a face. "That's how it appears."

"After all these years, Warren still worries I'll do something stupid, create political problems for the DA's Office. He treats me like a rookie."

"I don't think that's the case. From what I've seen, you're basically his right-hand woman. He trusts you with all the most important murder cases. He defers to your judgment constantly, and seeks it out."

"In the courtroom, yeah. But outside the courtroom, it's a different story. All I want is a chance to make sure Kelly Lee's accident was really an accident."

"Don't you see Warren's perspective, though?"

Jessie put down her cup. "What?"

"I'm just saying, especially in today's climate, police misconduct claims are extremely serious."

Jessie felt anger rise inside her. She'd expected support from Leary. Maybe even help. He wasn't a yes-man, blindly loyal to the city. He was a seeker of justice, like she was.

"That's not relevant to whether her death should be thoroughly investigated," she said.

"No, of course not. But from Warren's point of view—"

"And besides that, don't you think there's a need for lawyers like Kelly to keep the police honest? You think that all these claims she handled were frivolous? That all she was doing was trying to cash in on the PPD's bank account?"

Leary let go of her hand and straightened in his chair. "All I'm saying is that Warren probably has good reasons for not wanting to involve the DA'a office."

"I can't believe you're taking his side on this."

"I'm not saying I take his side. Just that I understand where he's coming from."

"I guess you understand where the AID investigators are coming from, too. And Emily."

Leary sighed. "You know I'm not the PPD's number one fan. And when I was a cop, I saw some activity that would probably be considered misconduct. I would never deny that. But bringing these lawsuits, asking for millions of dollars? What does that accomplish? It just drains money and resources that should be spent fighting crime and making Philadelphia safe."

"What it accomplishes is to make sure the police follow the law and the Constitution. Otherwise, we would have a totalitarian police state. It might be safe, but it wouldn't be a place where you want to live."

"That's law school stuff. This is the real world."

The words came like a slap to the face. All she could do was stare at him. "You don't believe that, Leary."

"Warren is just trying to maintain good relations between the DA's Office and the police department. It's not personal." Leary looked away, seeming to avoid her gaze. She sensed there was something he wasn't saying.

"What's this really about?" she said.

He started to respond, then stopped. He let out a breath. "I'm trying to help you."

"Really? It doesn't feel that way."

"You love being a prosecutor. You love the DA's Office. I don't want you to do something impulsive and jeopardize all of that for a woman you barely knew."

Jessie leaned back in her chair, finally understanding. "You think you're protecting me from myself."

"I just don't want you to—"

"Do you have any idea how incredibly condescending that is, Leary?"

He put his hands up. "I'm not being condescending."

"Believe it or not, I'm actually a highly competent, intelligent woman capable of rational thinking."

"I know that. I love you for that. I just don't want you to make a mistake—"

"You mean you don't want me to make the same mistake *you* made?"

His face fell and he looked down at his hands. Jessie felt a rush of regret. What she'd said had been a low blow. She knew the loss of his career as a homicide detective still caused him great pain. But she couldn't take the words back. She was so angry, she wasn't sure she would take them back even if she could.

"Emily and Warren want nothing to do with this." She shook her head, feeling her anger give way to frustration and sadness. "I thought I could count on you to be the one person who would support me no matter what. Obviously, I was wrong."

"Jessie...."

She got up from her chair. "I need to get back to the office."

8

BACK IN THE quiet stillness of her office, Jessie closed her eyes and let a wave of emotions sweep through her. She felt anger and sadness, but mostly a strange mixture of responsibility and guilt. Kelly Lee had come to her for help. Now Kelly was dead. Could Jessie have done something to save her?

Maybe. Maybe not. Agonizing over what had happened wasn't going to change it.

Her cell phone buzzed on her desk. She glanced at the screen, expecting to see Leary's name, but it wasn't Leary. It was Emily Graham.

She took a deep breath before answering. "Hey, Emily."

"Hey." There was a coldness, a distance in her friend's voice that brought an ache to Jessie's chest.

Could Jessie say something to mend things? "About yesterday...."

Graham cut her off. "Unless you're about to tell me you're going to walk away from this Kelly Lee thing, just stop talking."

Jessie stopped talking.

"That's what I thought." She heard Graham's sigh through the phone. "I'm calling because I thought you'd want to know, the ME was able to identify the driver in the wreck based on fingerprints recovered from the body."

"Kelly?"

"Yes."

There was a silence on the line, and Jessie sensed her friend's hesitation. "Is there more?" Jessie said.

"The accident investigation team didn't find any evidence that the accident was caused intentionally. No tampering with the vehicle, no trace of a bomb or other explosive. All police resources have been pulled from the case. There isn't going to be any further investigation."

Jessie's grip tightened around her phone. "I see."

"I know you were hoping for more."

"It hasn't even been twenty-four hours."

"I'm just telling you what AID told me."

"Kelly reported a threat against her. There's a company and a person with motive to hurt her. Come on."

"Look, Jessie, I tried to explain this to you. There's no sympathy for Kelly Lee within the department. No one is interested in going the extra mile on this one. That's just the way it is."

"You don't sound too broken up about it."

"I already told you why."

"That wasn't personal, Emily. Representing clients was her job. She's entitled to the same diligence as any other victim in Philadelphia. What she did for a living, any cases she brought against the police department—or you—none of that is relevant."

"This conversation is pointless. I called to give you the information, because I'm your friend, but—"

"I'm your friend, too. You know that, right, Emily?"

There was a pause. "I thought I did."

"Emily—"

"I know one thing. If some scumbag lawyer targeted you, I'd be on your side, one-hundred-percent."

"This isn't about sides." She could feel the arguments ready to pour from her mouth, but they were the same arguments she'd already made. She realized Graham was right—there was no point in continuing the debate. Nothing she said would convince Graham that Kelly Lee deserved the best efforts of the PPD—or Jessie.

"I need to run," Graham said.

"Okay."

Jessie ended the call and put away her phone. She leaned back in her chair, feeling miserable. Graham obviously felt betrayed, hurt, and that was something Jessie would need to address. But not by turning her back on Kelly Lee. Not by standing by and allowing an injustice to occur.

Fewer than twenty-four hours had passed since the accident, and the police had already ended their investigation. If Jessie didn't do something, no one else would.

But what could she do? Without the support of Graham, without any help from Leary, and without any authorization from Warren, she was alone.

She reached for the mouse and keyboard on her desk, then stopped and picked up her cell phone instead. Warren had prohibited her from "using the resources of this office" to get involved. Technically, if she relied on her own resources, she'd be complying with his commands.

Yeah, I'm sure that argument will carry a lot of weight when you're begging him not to fire you.

It was a chance she had to take. She opened the web browser on her phone. One Google search later, she had the phone number for Kelly's law office. She called it.

A woman's voice answered on the third ring. "Kelly Lee, Attorney at Law. This is her assistant, Cheyenne."

Jessie froze. There was something too businesslike, too matter-of-fact about the woman's tone. Had no one notified her of Kelly's death?

"My name is Jessica Black. I'm a prosecutor at the DA's Office, and also a friend of Kelly's. I.... Has anyone from the police department contacted you?"

"The police department? I don't know what this is about, but Kelly is not in the office at the moment. I'd be happy to take a message—"

"No, listen. I'm calling with some terrible news, Cheyenne. Kelly was in a car accident in Center City last night. A bad one." Jessie felt her throat constrict. "Kelly is dead."

She heard the assistant's sharp intake of breath. "Oh no."

"I'm sorry."

"Oh my God."

"Cheyenne, I'm calling because Kelly told me she was working on a big case—a class action lawsuit against a toy company. The client's name was...." She struggled to remember it.

"Rowland," Cheyenne said. "Ken and Deanna Rowland. Their son's name was Sam."

"You're familiar with the case?"

"All I know is Kelly was really passionate about it. She said it was her chance to do something good."

"She said something very similar to me. Are you at her office now, Cheyenne?"

"Why?"

"I'd like to see the Rowland file."

"I'm not sure if I'm allowed to give that to you."

"Please, it's...." Jessie hesitated, unsure how much to tell this woman she didn't know. "I'm not sure the car accident was really an accident. Kelly confided in me that she felt threatened. She thought someone might be following her. And she thought it was because of the Rowland case."

"Yeah, she said the same thing to me. She told me to be careful."

"It would be really helpful if I could see that file."

"Look, don't take this the wrong way. You sound legit. But the police have a history of calling here and trying to get information they're not supposed to have."

Jessie felt her jaw tense. "I'm not the police. I'm a lawyer, like Kelly."

"You're a prosecutor. To me, that doesn't sound much different than the police."

"Okay. I understand your concern. How about this? If the Rowlands authorize you to give me their file, would that make you comfortable?"

She held her breath as Cheyenne seemed to think it over. "I guess so."

"Can you give me their contact information? I'll talk to them right now."

Cheyenne seemed to hesitate again, but then she gave Jessie a phone number and address.

Five minutes later, Jessie headed out of the DA's Office, careful to avoid Warren Williams.

9

JESSIE RETRIEVED her car from its Center City garage and drove out to Devon, Pennsylvania, a town that was part of Philadelphia's Main Line suburbs. The tall buildings and city streets of Philly gave way to green lawns—slightly brown from the autumn chill—and large single-family homes.

The residential sections of Devon looked like sets from a movie, with neat fences, basketball hoops mounted above garage doors, and bikes and skateboards in the driveways. As the GPS app on her phone directed her to the address Kelly Lee's assistant had given her, she couldn't help imagining living in a town like this one day. Raising a family. The thought brought a warm feeling to her chest, but the feeling quickly soured as she realized Deanna and Ken Rowland had probably moved here for similar reasons.

She parked in front of their white colonial-style house and rang the doorbell. Within seconds, the door flung open and two hopeful faces stared out at her. Ken and Deanna Rowland were stoop-shouldered and disheveled, but she could see determination in their eyes. Deanna, as if afraid to speak, invited her inside with a wave of her hand.

She followed the couple into their house, walking past a foyer to a family room. There were toys strewn on the carpet. For a moment, Jessie wondered if the couple had more than one child. But the silence of the house told her that was probably not the case. More likely, the couple had not found the strength to clean up their son's belongings. Jessie felt emotion rise in her chest again. She forced herself to breathe. She was here to help these people, she reminded herself, and she could only do that if she remained professional.

"Thank you for seeing me on short notice," she said.

Deanna gestured for Jessie to sit on the couch, then sat down herself. She folded her hands in her lap and leaned forward. She looked frail and tentative. Her husband did not sit down. He paced back and forth in front of sliding glass doors facing the backyard.

"I'm sorry," Deanna Rowland said. "It's still hard for us to talk about Sam. That's why you said you wanted to see us, right? To talk to us about our case?"

"Yes. I'm an assistant district attorney with the Philadelphia DA's Office."

"Are you thinking about bringing criminal charges against that horrible company?" Ken Rowland said. There was a sudden energy in his voice that belied his slumped appearance.

Jessie shifted uneasily on the couch. "Actually, I'm here because I need to tell you some bad news. Your lawyer, Kelly Lee, died last night. She was in a car accident."

Deanna Rowland's hand flew to her mouth. Across the room, her husband stopped pacing, turned, and gaped at Jessie. "What?"

"Oh my God," Deanna Rowland said. "Oh no. Dear God."

"Why are you here to tell us?" Ken Rowland said. "Why you, an assistant DA?"

"I was Kelly's friend."

"Is that the only reason?" he said. "Do you think there could have been ... what's the word ... foul play?"

"What are you talking about, Ken?" Deanna Rowland said. But by the way the color drained from her face, Jessie suspected she understood exactly what her husband was suggesting.

"Do you think that's a realistic possibility?" Jessie said, turning the question around.

Ken Rowland did not hesitate. "Definitely."

"The AID—that's the Accident Investigation Division of the Philadelphia Police Department—didn't find anything suspicious at the scene," Jessie said.

"That company, and that man, Douglas Shaw—they have no morals." Ken Rowland crossed the room to stand near Jessie and his wife. "Do you know that they tried to pay us off? They offered us money to abandon the lawsuit. Of course, we would've had to agree to a nondisclosure agreement. They don't want anyone to know their toys kill children."

"They must have issued a recall," Jessie said.

"A recall?" Ken Rowland snorted a laugh. "No. All they did was stop selling the toys, and they issued a press release claiming a supply shortage. They denied everything about the toys being dangerous. That's how immoral these people are. They don't care about human life. They're scum."

Jessie let him talk, and hoped doing so had some therapeutic value. As a prosecutor who dealt with victims and their families on a regular basis, she had learned over the years to be not only a lawyer, but a kind of therapist as well. She did not try to counsel people—there were social workers and victims' advocates who performed that role better than she could—but she tried to be a good listener, to let them know she cared.

"I hear what you're saying," she said, choosing her words with care. "But you have to remember corporations aren't people. They always try to minimize costs and maximize profits.

From what I understand, settling with a litigant and demanding secrecy as part of the settlement isn't unusual. I'm not sure it's evidence of murderous intent."

"Kelly was afraid," Deanna Rowland said. "You claim you were her friend. Did she tell you she was afraid that someone was following her?"

"Yes." Thinking about their conversation in the criminal courthouse brought Jessie a fresh twinge of regret. "That's part of the reason I'm here. I want to make sure her concerns are looked into and taken seriously."

"You seem like a good person," Deanna Rowland said. "Were you and Kelly close?"

"We were friends in law school. We drifted apart after that. I wish we had stayed closer." Jessie pushed away the thought. "What about you? Has anyone threatened you?"

Deanna Rowland took a deep breath. "Not exactly. I mean, we never felt like anyone was following us. But when we rejected their settlement offer, they were angry. They told Kelly we would never win, and that they would bury us in legal fees before we even had a chance. They said we were making a huge mistake we would regret for the rest of our lives."

Ken Rowland sat down next to his wife and put his arm around her. "Deanna and I knew the only thing we would regret would be not going forward with the trial, not fighting for Sam. That's why we told them to take their hush money and shove it."

"If Kelly's dead, what happens to our case?" Deanna Rowland asked. "Who will be our lawyer now?"

"I'm not sure," Jessie said. "One of the reasons I'm here, actually, is to ask you to give Kelly's assistant permission to share your file with me."

"Are you going to take over our case?" Deanna Rowland said, her voice hopeful.

"No. As a prosecutor, I can't do that."

"Then why do you want access to our file?" Ken Rowland said.

"I want to see if there's anything in it that would shed light on Kelly's death."

Ken and Deanna exchanged a glance. "We'll give you access," Ken Rowland said, "but only if you promise us that you'll find us another lawyer—someone good—to handle our case."

Jessie hesitated. She knew Kelly Lee was a sole practitioner who had no partners or other lawyers working with her, but she had not anticipated the Rowlands asking her to find substitute counsel. She considered whether this was a promise she should commit to. Getting even more involved in Kelly Lee's affairs seemed like a bad idea given the pressure she was under to stay away, but the thought of the Rowlands' case being abandoned—or mishandled—was worse. Also, agreeing to their request might be her only way to get access to their file.

"Okay," she said. "I'll find another attorney to step in."

Ken Rowland nodded. "Thank you. I'll let Cheyenne know we're okay with you having a copy of the file."

"Can you call her now?"

"I'll call her," Ken Rowland said, "after we have a new lawyer."

Jessie forced her jaw to relax. "I'll go take care of that now."

How exactly she was going to do that, she wasn't sure.

10

THE LOBBY of Big Fitness was plain, unimpressive. Faded beige paint covered the walls, and the closest thing to decoration was a line of framed posters—photos of men and women exercising that looked like they'd been taken at least a decade ago. When Emily Graham showed her badge at the front desk, the woman sitting behind the counter, a young black woman wearing a Polo-style shirt bearing the gym's logo—jerked upright. "Is there some kind of situation?"

"No." Graham put away her badge. "I just need to talk to someone here, a friend."

"I heard about a guy in Delaware, walked into a gym with a machete in his bag and hacked up two other guys in the locker room."

"It's nothing like that," Graham said. She glanced around, wondering if that sort of thing happened here. The place might be drab, but it didn't look *that* bad. "I'm a detective. I need to talk to another detective, who happens to be a member here."

The girl seemed to relax. "That's a relief. Go ahead in."

She proceeded to the weight room. The temperature seemed ten degrees warmer, and the odors of rubber and sweat were palpable. People—mostly men—moved among the machines and free weights. Someone dropped a large weight and it hit the mat with a loud thud. She scanned the room until she found the man she'd come to see.

AID Detective Ross Reid, the lead investigator on the Kelly Lee automobile accident, sat on a bench, a dumbbell gripped in his right hand, doing curls. His face was a grimace of concentration. Beads of sweat stood out on his forehead. His biceps muscle bulged.

She headed toward him and he looked up, seeing her. He let out a breath and placed the dumbbell next to his right sneaker.

"Detective Emily Graham." He watched her, didn't smile as he said her name. "Safe to say you're not here to work out, wearing that."

She was wearing her unofficial uniform, a dark gray pantsuit. "I heard this was the place to find you."

"From who?"

Graham sat beside him on the bench. It was awkward, but not as awkward as standing over him. "Can you talk for a minute?"

"Now? Here?"

"I wanted to talk to you off the record."

"Why?"

Good question. Graham wasn't really sure what she was doing here, and the thought of leaving was becoming more attractive by the second.

Reid picked up a towel and wiped his face. "You homicide detectives think you run the whole department."

"I don't think that."

"But you think you can disturb me during my personal time."

"I only need a couple minutes."

"Right. I'm sure."

She felt her fist clench in response to his sarcastic tone. She forced her hand to relax. "You concluded that there was no foul play in Kelly Lee's accident."

"That's what you want to talk about?"

Actually, it was the last thing on Earth she wanted to talk about, but she said, "I'm just surprised by how quickly your unit was able to close the investigation."

"Easy. There was nothing to investigate." He wiped his face again.

"But you're aware she was threatened shortly before the crash?"

Reid looked at her. His lip curled. "Did you seriously come here to question my investigation?"

"I'm not questioning it."

"She wasn't threatened. She told the police that she *felt* threatened. There's a difference."

Graham nodded. "That's true. Did you investigate that angle?"

"What angle? Her feelings?"

"Yes."

He stared at her for another few seconds—enough time for Graham to mentally ask herself again what the *hell* she was doing—and then he let out a derisive laugh. "I guess a brilliant homicide detective like you would have handled it differently, huh?"

"I didn't say that. I'm just asking."

"The bitch crashed. End of story."

Graham flinched. The reaction seemed to make Reid happy. He smirked at her.

"Why do you call her a bitch?" Graham said.

"You know why."

"You dislike her because of her lawsuits against the Department?"

"Of course. She hurt a lot of good cops."

"I know that." Graham debated confiding in him—the guy was certainly not a person she enjoyed talking to—but decided to do it in an attempt to establish rapport. "One of her police misconduct claims was about me."

"Really?" Reid turned slightly on the bench, facing her, and his expression softened. She was relieved to see the change.

"Even us brilliant homicide detectives aren't immune," she said.

"Was there any truth in the claim?"

"None at all."

"Department settled?"

Graham nodded. "That's how it works."

"Lawyers suck."

"A lot of them do," she said. "There are some decent ones out there."

Reid shook his head. "Few and far between, if you ask me."

"What about the explosion?" Graham said. "Lee lost control of the car, collided with a building. I get that. But then her car explodes? Her body parts go flying? That doesn't seem typical."

He turned away. "Maybe not typical, but that's what happened."

"You looked for evidence of some kind of bomb, or accelerant?"

"Why are you asking me these questions, Detective?"

"I want to know."

He shook his head. "There's nothing to know, okay? Lee died in an accident. Case closed."

"I understand, but did you look into possible causes for such a big explosion? You didn't answer my question."

"I don't have to answer your questions." He looked at the dumbbell at his feet, then lifted it, stood up, and returned it to the rack. Apparently he'd decided that his workout was over. He turned back to her. "You said this conversation is off the record."

"That's right."

"Good. Keep it that way. Trust me, we'll both be better off."

"What does that mean?"

He was already heading away from her, toward the door to the locker rooms. Either he didn't hear the question, or he chose not to respond.

11

FINDING a new lawyer for the Rowlands, when she didn't even have the case file or access to all of the facts, was not going to be easy. She decided her first stop should be the Court of Common Pleas, located inside City Hall, where the judge assigned to the Rowlands' case could tell her the status. Looking online, she found out that the judge was a woman named Cynthia Dax.

As a prosecutor, Jessie spent plenty of time in the hallways and courtrooms of Philadelphia's Juanita Kidd Stout Center for Criminal Justice—commonly referred to as the CJC—but she'd never practiced a day of civil litigation, so the Court of Common Pleas was foreign territory to her. She didn't know her way around, knew none of the staff, and had never met Judge Dax. She tried not to let any of this intimidate her as she made her way through the building's hallways.

Jessie knocked on the door of Judge Cynthia Dax's chambers. No one responded. She tried to look casual as she pressed her ear to the dark wood. She couldn't hear anything through the door. A few men in suits walked past her with suspicious glances. She straightened up, feeling awkward and self-conscious.

She knocked again. Maybe she should have tried to do this by phone, but it had seemed more appropriate to talk about Kelly's death face-to-face. She was considering what to do next when the judge's door swung open.

A woman emerged and almost bumped into Jessie. "Watch it. You're in my way." The woman strode past her.

"Wait. My name is Jessie Black." Jessie followed the billowing black robe, hurrying to catch up. "Judge Dax, please."

The judge stopped and turned. She had long, blonde hair that looked incongruously youthful framing her weathered, creased face. Her pale gray eyes seemed to regard Jessie with annoyance.

"I need to talk to you about the Rowland case."

The judge's expression seemed to harden. "I don't have time right now."

"I only need a few minutes. I was a friend of Kelly Lee. I'm not sure if you've heard about her accident."

"I'm sorry for your loss, but I really need to—"

"I've spoken with the Rowlands. I'm hoping you can bring me up to speed on the status of their lawsuit. We should discuss assigning them new counsel—"

"Lurking outside my chambers so you can ambush me in the hallway is hardly the right way to get assigned as their lawyer."

Jessie felt her frustration begin to build. "I'm an assistant DA. I'm not here looking to get assigned as counsel myself. I'm just here to find out the status and—"

"There is no status. I haven't ruled on either motion yet. Now, if you'll excuse me, I need to get going."

"Either motion?"

The judge let out a frustrated sigh. "Ms. Lee moved the Court to certify a class so that she could proceed with a class action lawsuit against the defendants. The defense opposed the motion and moved for summary judgment."

Jessie tried to absorb the information before Judge Dax could leave. She had almost no knowledge of the laws or procedures involved in a class action suit, but she knew generally how motion practice worked. "Did the parties submit briefs in support of these motions?"

Jessie figured that certifying a class must be one of the first steps in a class action suit, so the trial must still be at a very early stage. Kelly was seeking the court's approval to represent not just the Rowlands, but everyone harmed by Boffo's dangerous products, and Boffo was opposing the request. Boffo's motion for summary judgment was an attempt to get the whole case tossed out without a trial, on the basis that the Rowlands had no legitimate legal case. Reading the briefs would give Jessie a much better understanding of the case and help her pitch it to potential lawyers.

"You ask a lot of questions, Ms. Black." The judge resumed her march down the hallway. Jessie had to jog to keep up with her.

"When were the motions filed?"

"A few days ago."

"Did the parties present arguments at a hearing?"

"A hearing hasn't been scheduled yet."

"May I see the briefs in support of the motions?"

"No, you may not," Judge Dax said, rounding on her suddenly with an angry glare. "The pleadings have been sealed as confidential by motion of the defense. Now, like I said, I have somewhere important to be. I assume you do, too."

Jessie didn't understand the woman's hostility. She searched for the right words. "What about finding new legal counsel for the Rowlands?"

"That's their problem, isn't it? Maybe criminal defendants are entitled to free legal counsel, but personal injury plaintiffs are not."

"I didn't say *free*. I'm sure a lot of local lawyers would be interested in stepping in."

"I doubt it."

"The case sounded pretty strong when Kelly described it to me."

"I guess that's why I'm a judge and you're not."

The judge strode away, leaving Jessie even more stunned than before. What the judge had implied—that other lawyers wouldn't want to take on the Rowlands' case—seemed at odds with what Kelly had told her about the strength of the case against Boffo, but Jessie wasn't up to speed on the laws at issue. She was out of her depth.

At least she'd learned the basic status of the case. Walking out of City Hall, she mentally reviewed the lawyers she knew you might have the qualifications to take on the case.

12

THE TEMPERATURE outside City Hall had dropped, and Jessie felt a chill as she walked away from the entrance. She turned away from the traffic, pressed her phone to her ear, and called a personal injury lawyer named Bud Derren, whom she'd heard speak at a legal conference a few months before.

"I'm the one who complained about the lack of coffee," she reminded him.

"I remember you." His voice sounded chipper. "How can I help?"

"I don't know if you heard, but Kelly Lee was recently in a fatal car accident."

"I did hear that." The sounds of the city around her made hearing difficult, but she thought a note of sadness in his voice.

"I'm trying to help some of her clients find new counsel." She gave him a brief summary of the Rowlands' claims.

"I'm going to pass," Derren said.

"Pass? Why?"

"My docket is really full at the moment."

"Too full for a case where you bring down a powerful

company harming children? Think of the free advertising, if nothing else."

A car horn blocked out his response. Jessie took a few steps away from the busy street and pressed her phone harder against her ear. "Sorry," she said. "I'm outside. Can you say that again?"

"Why are you outside?"

She thought about Warren's admonition not to interfere in the Kelly Lee matter and felt a twinge of misgiving, as if she were sneaking around—which she supposed she was. "Just multitasking," she said vaguely.

"I said, it's not about publicity. Believe me, I love kids and if it was in my power, I would punish every company and person who dared to put money ahead of a child's well-being. But what you need to understand is that I practice personal injury law on a contingent fee basis. My firm invests thousands—often tens of thousands—of its own money in a case, but we only get paid if we win, because our fees ultimately come out of a damages verdict or a settlement. Taking a case is like making a bet, and to survive in my world you need to be a savvy gambler. If I had the confidence that this case was a good bet—or just an even bet for that matter—I'd jump on it. But going up against a company with a huge war chest, before a judge like Judge Dax? I'm not going to take a bet like that."

Jessie's chest tightened. Hearing a respected lawyer describe the adjudication of the legal rights of grieving parents as gambling and betting disturbed her, but she pushed aside her distaste. What mattered was helping the Rowlands. "Is there anyone you can think of who would be a good match for this case?"

"I can give you a few names, but don't get your hopes up."

His warning was apt, and her other calls were similarly unsuccessful. No one seemed interested in picking up the Rowlands' case. The local personal injury lawyers were familiar with Judge Cynthia Dax, who was apparently known to be sympathetic to corporate defendants. The deep pockets of Boffo Products Corporation didn't make the scenario any more appealing. No one she spoke with seemed to think taking the case would be a smart business move.

The conversations left Jessie feeling confused. When she and Kelly had spoken, Kelly had made it sound like the Rowlands' case was a sure thing, but now it seemed Kelly had been taking a big chance on the Rowlands. She remembered something Kelly had said. *The Rowlands' case is different. Do you understand? The Rowland case is a chance for me to actually do something good.*

Out of other options, Jessie took a deep breath and called the only other personal injury lawyer she could think of. Noah Snyder.

The aging, silver-haired lawyer had been a thorn in Jessie's side more often than he'd been an ally, but she knew him to be smart, resourceful, and, most importantly, non-discriminating. He handled criminal matters, personal injury claims, workers compensation cases, trusts and estates, and anything else that walked through the door of his low-rent legal practice carrying a checkbook or a credit card. He rented space in a shoddy building a few blocks from the criminal courthouse, where he employed a slew of young associates whose only common trait was an inability to find a better job. He worked these people to the bone while paying them the bare minimum and doing as little work as possible himself.

But Jessie had seen him negotiate excellent plea agreements for criminal clients. She'd been on the other side of several of those negotiations and had been surprised as he outmaneuvered her. She knew he preferred settling to trying cases, but he had no qualms sending his underlings into court. If she could interest anyone in picking up the Rowlands' case, it might be Snyder. She had no choice now but to try.

"Jessie Black." The sound of his voice made her instantly question her decision to call him, but there was no turning back now. "Do I have a case pending against you? I don't remember—"

"No, actually. I need to talk to you about something else."

"Sure, what is it? I hope you're not fundraising because I don't.... Hold on a sec." She heard voices on the other end of the line and realized she didn't have his full attention.

"Are you in your office, Noah? Let me come visit you. We can discuss this in person."

"Discuss what?"

"I'll be there soon."

Ten minutes later, Snyder's receptionist, a pleasant woman named Danielle, greeted her in the lobby. She buzzed Snyder. He arrived a moment later with a smirk she was all too familiar with. "Never thought I'd see you inside my humble headquarters, Black. Want a tour?"

She had not come to sightsee, but figured, what the hell? She'd always been curious about this place. "Sure, Noah."

He led her from the lobby into an open-floor environment where his worker bees crouched in tiny cubicles cranking away at their cases. The windows were closed to the autumn chill, and the stuffy air reeked of printer toner, fast food, and sweat. Jessie felt bad for the lawyers here, who'd fought their way through law school only to wind up slaving away in this dungeon. Snyder ushered her into his own office, and it was like stepping into a completely different building.

While Snyder had furnished the majority of his "humble headquarters" with cheap, industrial office furniture, he'd lavished money and attention on his own office, which was luxurious and beautiful. He walked behind a huge mahogany desk and dropped into a leather swivel chair. He gestured at the two visitor chairs and Jessie sat in one. These were leather as well, and very comfortable. As her body sank into the leather, she imagined that Snyder had wooed many a potential client in this chair, impressing and pampering them before handing their cases off to one of the minions in the cubicle farm to arrange a quick settlement. A feeling of doubt began to creep into her mind. Had coming here been a bad idea?

"Scotch?" Snyder said.

"Excuse me?" It was barely after noon.

"Cigar?" Snyder tapped a humidor on the corner of his desk. "Cuban. The good stuff."

"No thanks."

"Do you mind if I have one?"

"Yeah, kind of."

Snyder seemed to find this amusing. "Fine. But the Scotch is twenty-five-year single malt. I'm not letting you turn me down on that. It's too great an insult."

He set two glasses on his desk and leaned sideways to open one of the desk drawers. He withdrew a bottle and filled both glasses with brown liquid. A powerful smell filled the air. Snyder pushed one of the glasses across the desk to her and raised his own in a toast. Jessie hesitated, then picked up her glass and clinked it with his.

She sipped. Scotch was not her thing—she wasn't much of a drinker, other than an occasional glass of wine—but she had to admit it went down pretty smoothly. "It's good."

"Good? That's a five-hundred dollar bottle of Balvenie."

"I'm flattered you would share it with me."

Snyder drained his glass in one long swallow, then refilled it. He sighed contentedly and leaned back in his chair with the fresh drink in his hand. "So why are you here?"

"I have a potential referral for you."

He laughed, coughing up some of his drink. "No, seriously."

"I am serious." She told him about Kelly's death, then laid out the Rowlands' case in as much detail as possible—which wasn't much, since Judge Dax had not given her access to the pleadings. She also told him what the Rowlands had told her— Boffo's attempt to settle the case, their anger when the Rowlands refused. She finished by recapping her meeting with Judge Dax.

"Dax is a real bitch," he said.

Jessie waited for him to continue. Snyder slowly finished his drink. "And?" she said.

"I appreciate you thinking of me for this case. Although I'm pretty sure I wasn't your first choice." He offered her a knowing smile. "I'm not interested."

"Why not?"

"Tell me why everyone else turned you down."

Jessie sighed. "They all thought the chances of winning were too low."

Snyder let out a snort. "What a bunch of pussies."

His crude tone made her stiffen. "What's *your* reason?"

"You lost me when you told me the Rowlands refused to even consider a settlement offer. I like clients who settle. Quick and easy, money for everybody. The last thing I want to do is go to some musty old courtroom and drone on in front of a judge and a jury, and talk to a bunch of boring expert witnesses. How would my girlfriend put it? *Ain't nobody got time for dat shit.*"

"I don't think I've met your girlfriend. She sounds interesting."

"She's a peach. The bottom line is, from what I'm hearing, the Rowlands want a courtroom showdown. I don't go in for that Perry Mason shit."

"So it's not the thought of losing that bothers you. It's the thought of working."

"Well, when you put it that way, it sounds...." He considered. "True."

"Sometimes if you go to trial, the award can be larger than a settlement. Isn't that true? Think about it. You could take a settlement offer from a company like Boffo, or you could beat them on the merits and let a jury decide how much they should have to pay. The Rowlands retained Kelly on a contingency basis. I'm sure they would do the same with you. You would take a percentage of the damages verdict, which could be substantial, and make a difference in the world by putting companies like Boffo on notice that endangering children won't be tolerated."

Snyder clapped. "This is why I share my good Scotch with you, Black. You're endlessly entertaining. "

She ignored the backhanded compliment. "I'm sure all the hard work has already been done by Kelly. The legal research, the expert reports, the initial filings. All you need to do is pick up her work, stroll into the courtroom, and wow them with your good looks and charm."

Snyder's smile widened. "I do have those in abundance."

"Beat a company like Boffo, and you'll be buying plenty more bottles of overpriced Scotch."

"It's not overpriced."

"Will you at least think about it?"

"Why do you care so much?"

"Because this is an important case."

"Why?"

"Because a child—"

"Why is it important to *you*?"

"That is why."

Snyder rocked back in his chair and watched her with a knowing smirk. "I'll need to see the file before I agree. Make sure all the annoying legal work is already done, like you say."

Jessie hesitated. She needed to call the Rowlands. "Do you have a spare conference room where I can make a call?"

He put on a hurt expression. "Why not call from here? Are you trying to hide something from me?"

Jessie took a deep breath and forced a smile. "Of course not, Noah. Here is fine."

13

JESSIE CALLED the Rowlands while Noah Snyder poured himself a third glass of Scotch.

"I think I found a lawyer to take your case." She ignored Snyder's arched eyebrow.

Over the phone line, she heard Deanna say, "Great! Thank you so much...."

Ken, who was also on the line, cut in. "What do you mean, 'think'?"

"He needs to see Kelly's files before he can make a final decision." It wasn't the whole truth, but it wasn't exactly a lie, either. "Will you please call Cheyenne and authorize her to show us your case file?"

There was silence on the line. She heard a hum of hesitation from Ken as he presumably mulled over her request.

"Oh for God's sake, Ken, why not?" Deanna said.

"Okay," Ken said. "We'll call her."

The call disconnected. Jessie waited.

"So you haven't seen Kelly Lee's file," Snyder observed.

"Not yet, but the Rowlands are arranging for us to have access."

"Why do I get the feeling you have an ulterior motive for being here?"

Jessie shrugged. "No idea. Maybe because you drink too much?"

Even though his gaze had become watery, she could feel him scrutinizing her. "You genuinely care about the case," he said. "I know you well enough to believe that. But there's something else going on here, too."

"There's nothing else, Noah."

"You want to see her files, and not just to prove to me that taking over the case will be a cake-walk. I know there's more going on here than Jessica Black, good Samaritan, trying to play matchmaker between an orphaned client and Philadelphia's least-respected attorney-at-law. You're using me, but I'm not sure to what end."

"There's no mystery. I really am a good Samaritan."

Snyder laughed as if she were an endless source of delight for him. It was getting harder to throttle her urge to smack the smug look off his face.

"You know what I think, Jess? I think that you think your friend Kelly Lee was murdered. And I think your boss, the great and mighty Warren Williams—who hates me, by the way, so you might not want to mention my name to him—doesn't want you sticking your nose into a case the PPD wants to bury. But you're doing it anyway, on your own time. Tell me if I'm hot or cold."

All she could do was glare at him.

He grinned back at her. "I think you're using me as cover. An opportunity to see Kelly Lee's files without actually doing it yourself and getting fired. Come on, tell me I'm right. I never get tired of hearing it."

She chewed her lip. She didn't trust Snyder and didn't want to tell him anything he could later use against her. "I don't know if Kelly's death was really an accident. That's a question for the police. I'm just trying to help the Rowlands."

Her phone vibrated, saving her from the discussion. Ken Rowland said, "Cheyenne will meet you at Kelly's office. You know where that is?"

"The Gardner Building, right?"

"When will our lawyer get in touch with us? What's his name?"

"Soon."

Jessie disconnected. "Do you have a car here? Mine's in a garage."

"Wait a second. You think I'm going with you? I've got appointments." He reached for the bottle of Scotch. It was empty.

"Maybe we should take a cab."

"Maybe *you* should take a cab. Bring me the file."

Jessie hesitated. "I don't—"

"Let me guess. You want me to go with you because Warren told you to stay out of this. Because he doesn't want you looking into ... what did you call it? Something that should be a question for the police."

She winced. "Will you come with me or not?"

He sighed, as if the fifteen minute trip would be an immense undertaking. "I guess I can move my calendar around."

They caught a cab and took it across town. The Gardner Building, an impressively tall office tower, was one of several in this area of Philly, which was dominated by the even taller towers of One and Two Liberty Place. According to a plaque on the Gardner Building's brick façade, the other tenants ranged from a small marketing agency to the Philly office of a global accounting firm.

A food truck tempted her with the smells of grilled steak, cheese, onions, and peppers. She considered indulging. She was hungry. But she didn't want to wolf down a cheesesteak in front of Snyder. Some activities could not be performed gracefully, and eating a cheesesteak on the sidewalk was one of them.

Not that Snyder was paying her any attention. The silver-haired lawyer was looking at his reflection in the glass and chrome storefront of one of the neighboring buildings, fixing the knot of his tie.

The squeal of air brakes distracted her as a city bus pulled to a stop and disgorged a stream of men and women. Most of them headed for the Gardner Building's entrance.

"You know, I looked at office space in this shithole," Snyder said. "Total ripoff."

Snyder was calling this place a shithole? That was a joke, given his own HQ. "The good news is you can work on the case from your own lovely office," she said.

There was an impish glint in his eye. "I still haven't agreed to work on the case at all."

"But you're here."

He laughed and shook his head. "I'm still not exactly sure why."

"Because deep down inside, you're a good lawyer dedicated to our noble profession?"

"Definitely *not* that."

Jessie opened the door for him, since it didn't look like he was going to do the honors. He strolled past her into the building's lobby.

"Unless we find some kind of magical documents that guarantee success on a massive scale, I think we're both going to be leaving here disappointed." His voice echoed in the large, marble-laden lobby. "However, I will be less disappointed than you, because there's an excellent cigar store down the street, and this outing gives me a nice opportunity to check in and see their new stock."

She didn't give him the satisfaction of a response. They stepped into one of the elevators, along with two men in business suits. Jessie touched the number for Kelly Lee's floor. The doors slid closed and the car ascended.

They stood in awkward silence, Snyder tapping one Italian shoe against the floor of the elevator car and humming tunelessly. The elevator made a rattling, clanging sound as it ascended. Snyder arched an eyebrow. "Told you this place was a shithole. Maybe I'm wrong and we won't leave disappointed. Maybe we won't leave at all."

The two businessmen gave him wary looks.

"We'll be fine," Jessie said.

"Hey, maybe we should look into a class action lawsuit against the elevator company."

"One thing at a time."

"You still dating that cop?"

"What?"

"The homicide detective you banged in the alleyway?"

The two businessmen made a valiant effort to pretend they weren't listening. Jessie felt her face and neck flush. She gritted her teeth. "I don't see how my personal life is any of your business."

"I'm just making conversation. I like you. I want to know more about you."

The elevator jerked to a stop. The doors opened and the two businessmen hurried out. She wished she could follow them. When the doors slid closed again and the elevator resumed its climb, she was alone with Snyder.

"Why don't you tell me about *your* love life?" she said.

Snyder shrugged. "Sure. Sharing is caring, right? I'm single at the moment."

"What about your girlfriend? The one who says, *Ain't nobody got time for dat shit?*"

Snyder burst out laughing. "For the record, no matter what else happens, even if we plummet to our deaths in this elevator, everything was worth it just to hear you say that."

"Glad I could entertain you."

"But back to you. Bumping uglies in an unmarked police car in an alleyway? I'm very envious. I think that's much more impressive than any of your courtroom victories."

"How about if we focus on the case?"

"Sure thing. Why do you think she was murdered? Did her ghost appear to you, *Hamlet*-style?"

"I never said I think she was murdered."

"That was a Shakespeare reference by the way. I'm very cultured. And you definitely think she was murdered. You wouldn't be here otherwise."

"Her assistant's name is Cheyenne." The elevator chimed and the doors opened with a hiss. "Try to be respectful, okay? The woman's boss just died."

"When am I anything less?"

14

SNYDER STROLLED out of the elevator and headed for Kelly Lee's office suite. Jessie followed him, annoyed to have to jog in his wake. Snyder grasped the knob and they walked inside. There was a small waiting room for clients, with chairs, a couch, and a reception desk. A young woman with bright, blue hair and skintight jeans leaned against the desk. Snyder came up short. "Oh."

Jessie had to struggle not to roll her eyes. At least now, maybe there was something about the case that Snyder would find interesting.

"You must be Cheyenne. I'm Jessie. This is Noah Snyder, the lawyer who's going to take over the Rowland case."

"*Might* take over," Snyder said.

"Thanks for coming," Cheyenne said. "Kelly kept her files in her office. Through that door." She pointed. "I'll be in here, gathering up my stuff. Let me know if you need anything."

"I guess you're out of a job, huh?" Snyder said. His eyes seemed to sweep up and down her body at regular intervals. Apparently, he'd forgotten his assurances to be respectful, assuming he even knew what the word meant.

"It looks that way," Cheyenne said.

"I might be able to give you some work."

Cheyenne shot Jessie a look, and Jessie tugged Snyder toward the office before he could creep her out even more. "Come on, Noah."

They passed through the doorway from the lobby to Kelly's office. At first glance, it appeared to be a typical lawyer's lair, with furniture straight out of a high-end office catalog, diplomas and bar certificates, on the walls, and a bookshelf. But on closer inspection, the bookshelf only held a handful of law books. Most of the shelves were dominated by books Jessie didn't recognize. She scanned the spines, seeing titles about game theory, poker, betting, acting, selling, and negotiation.

"I have this one," Snyder said. He pulled a thick volume off the shelf. "It was written by a hacker who used social engineering to get access to all kinds of secure information. Great tips about how to make people trust and believe you."

"I usually do that by telling the truth."

Snyder shook his head. "Looks like Kelly Lee didn't share your moral limitations."

"Kelly *was* moral. That's why the Rowlands' case was so important to her."

"Yeah, that and millions of dollars."

Jessie bit her lip. She was here to learn what had happened to Kelly, not to judge her.

Snyder walked around the office and opened a few cabinets. Jessie glimpsed office supplies. "Not a bottle of liquor to be seen," he said, opening another cabinet. "Not even one of those little travel-size ones."

"Haven't you had enough today?"

"Never. And look at this chair." He came around her desk and set the swivel chair spinning. "Her poor back."

The chair looked normal enough to Jessie. She gripped the

back to stop its movement. "We're not here to drink or relax, Noah." She sat in the chair and started opening drawers in the desk. "We're here to review the Rowland file."

"You really think I'm going to hang out here with you and read?" Snyder's expression was incredulous.

"Why else did you come here with me?"

"I'm asking myself the same question."

Jessie found nothing in the drawers. She got up and walked to a filing cabinet on one of the walls. She opened the top drawer. "Well, I'm sorry to bore you."

"Oh, you could never bore me, Jessie."

She let out a frustrated breath. "I can't find the Rowland file. It doesn't look like *any* of Kelly's case files are here. All I'm finding are bills, invoices, that sort of thing. Can you help me please?"

"Maybe we should ask the hot girl."

Before Jessie could respond, Snyder was out the door and back to the suite's lobby. Jessie waited, her frustration mounting as the sound of his voice drifted back to her through the doorway. *What was I thinking, going to Noah Snyder?* After what felt like an eternity, he returned with Cheyenne, Snyder smiling and the assistant looking like she wanted to crawl out of her own skin. Jessie had to force her jaw to relax.

"Let me take a look," Cheyenne said. She looked inside the filing cabinet drawer Jessie had opened. Her brow furrowed as she flipped past folders of what looked like bank statements. Quickly, she checked the other drawers in the filing cabinet and then the drawers in Kelly's desk. "I don't understand. This is so weird."

"What's weird?" Jessie said.

"Kelly's client files. They're gone."

Jessie felt a prickling sensation at the back of her neck. "You know that for sure?"

"I know where she kept her client files. The Rowlands' file should be in this drawer." She tapped the bottom drawer of the filing cabinet with her shoe. "It's gone, along with the other ones."

Jessie and Snyder exchanged a glance. "What about digital files?" Snyder said. Everyone turned toward the computer on the desk. Cheyenne nodded, went to the computer, and turned it on. Jessie and Snyder waited as she logged in. "Crap. The digital files are gone, too. Like somebody deleted them."

"Did Kelly keep backups?" Jessie said.

Cheyenne shook her head doubtfully. "Once in a while she took copies home with her to work on at her apartment. You might find something there. But she didn't have any official backups or anything like that."

Snyder spread his arms. "So, basically, all the work she supposedly did on the case is lost. Whoever takes over the case for the Rowlands—a person who will now most definitely not be me—is in for a whole lot of legal and factual research, drafting, and investment in experts. Sucks for them."

"You can't let this case die," Jessie said. "Please, Noah."

He shook his head. "I may be a cool guy, but unlike you, I'm not a good Samaritan." He walked out of the office. Without turning, he called over his shoulder, "Call me if you want that job, Cheyenne."

The assistant looked at Jessie. "What are you going to do?"

Jessie wasn't sure.

15

THE TAXI PULLED to a stop in front of Kelly Lee's apartment building. Jessie paid the driver and climbed out. Standing on the sidewalk, she looked up at the building. The ten-story building was plain and brown, like a dozen other ones in the Center City area. Ranks of identical windows faced the street.

She entered a generic-looking lobby. There was an elevator bank, an alcove with the tenants' mailboxes, and a door marked *Office*. The door was open, and when she leaned inside, she saw a pudgy Indian man sitting at a desk.

"Hi. Are you the building manager?"

He rose from his chair and extended a hand. "Are you looking for an apartment? My name is Nishith."

"Actually, I'm hoping you can let me into someone else's apartment."

Nishith's face creased with concern. Jessie hesitated for a second, thinking of Warren's commandment, but then showed the man her DA's Office ID. The fact that all of Kelly's client files were missing was proof that the accident was not what it appeared, right? Warren would surely understand that.

"This is about the woman in 7D?" Nishith said. "Ms. Lee, yes?"

Jessie nodded. "Did you know her?"

"Only to say hi in the elevator. She seemed like a nice woman. Very busy."

"If you could let me inside her apartment, that would be very helpful."

"Yes." He unlocked a drawer in his file cabinet, flipped through some files, and retrieved a manila folder. His hand disappeared into the folder and came out holding a key. "Come with me."

He led her to the elevator bank. Together they rode to the seventh floor. In the hallway, Jessie spotted Kelly Lee's door. 7D.

"That's strange," the building manager said.

"What?"

"Lights are on." He gestured at the door and Jessie saw what he'd noticed—a strip of light between the door and the floor. Someone had turned the lights on in Kelly's apartment.

"Have you given anyone else access?"

"No."

"Could the police be in there?"

"I doubt it. They said they had everything they need."

"Did Kelly give anyone else a key?"

"Not that I know of."

Jessie felt a tremor of fear. She reached for her phone, inwardly debating whether to call the police, but the building manager headed for the door before she could call anyone. "Nishith, hold on."

He stuck his key in the lock and turned. Cursing under her breath, Jessie hurried to join him as he opened the door.

Inside the apartment, two men turned to look at them. Jessie's body went cold. The men were dressed in black and wore gloves. One of them stood in front of a fancy wooden cabinet. The cabinet was open and one of his hands was inside it. The other man was looking at a bookshelf.

The men looked at each other. Some silent communication passed between them.

"Don't move," Jessie said. "I'm calling the police."

She fumbled with her phone, tapping 911 with a shaking finger and wishing she'd done it earlier. She heard Nishith cry out, and when she looked up from her phone, she saw the men charging toward them. She let out a scream of her own and dropped her phone, raising her hands protectively in front of her. The men ran past her, through the door and into the hallway. She swung around and watched them disappear into a stairwell.

"I don't understand." Nishith stared at the stairwell door, still rattling in its frame. "Were they burglars?"

"Worse."

She looked around her. Kelly's apartment was spotless. Common burglars would have trashed the place looking for valuables. These men had been careful not to disturb anything.

If Jessie and Nishith hadn't stumbled upon them, no one would ever know they'd been here.

———

LATER, Kelly Lee's apartment was filled with members of the police department. Emily Graham came with them.

"You have to agree it's looking more and more like Douglas Shaw and his company are behind all of this," Jessie said.

Graham picked up an expensive-looking vase from a shelf. "Behind all of what?"

"Come on, Emily."

"Does it bother you at all that bringing frivolous lawsuits

against good cops like me enabled your law school buddy to collect fine crystal?" Graham put down the vase.

"What bothers me is that a woman was murdered and the police refuse to investigate because of a personal grudge."

Graham's gaze swept the room, where police officers were checking out the apartment. "You keep saying that, but there's no evidence."

"No evidence? What about the two men I just caught searching her apartment?"

Graham shrugged. "It's depressingly common for burglars to target the homes of the recently deceased."

"This wasn't a burglary." Jessie felt rising frustration. "They didn't steal anything."

"Because you interrupted them in the act."

"They were looking for something. Probably the same thing I came here to look for. Kelly's files."

"Why?"

"To bury the Rowlands' case. To protect Douglas Shaw and his company." Jessie's body vibrated with anger. There was something wrong here. She didn't know if the police were simply blinded by their resentment of the police misconduct suits, or whether something even worse explained their inaction, but something was very wrong. "Maybe Douglas Shaw and Boffo bribed someone in the department."

"No way," Graham said. But Jessie thought she saw a flicker of doubt in her friend's eyes.

"How else do you explain the total lack of interest in Kelly's death?"

"I already explained it. There's no evidence that her death was anything other than a car accident."

"Excuse me." One of the cops had approached them. "We're done here," he said to Graham.

"Did you find anything?" Graham said.

"Lifted a few prints, but if the men were wearing gloves, I doubt they'll tell us anything."

"How can you be done?" Jessie stared at the man. "You've only been here ten minutes."

He shrugged. The other police were already leaving.

Jessie shook her head and turned to Graham. "I need to talk to Douglas Shaw."

"No, you don't."

"This isn't a game to me, Emily. He murdered a woman. I'm going to prove it."

"I need to get back to the Roundhouse," Graham said. "Why don't you come with me? I'll give you a ride to your office."

"First I need to look for Kelly's files."

"Jessie, this is a crime scene."

"No one else seems to think so."

The women faced each other. Jessie thought Graham might push the issue, but she didn't. She turned toward the door. "I guess I'll check in with you later, then."

"Fine."

Once Graham was gone, Jessie let out a sigh and looked around. The apartment was spacious, a two-bedroom apartment in which one of the bedrooms had been set up as a home office. All of the rooms were tastefully decorated, with an expensive touch as Graham had pointed out. Kelly had been doing well for herself. Among the artwork and sculptures, Jessie found a shelf of framed photographs—an elderly Asian man and woman, a family of four, also Asian, and a young man standing with a young woman. Jessie assume these people were Kelly's relatives, although Kelly herself did not appear in any of the pictures.

The home office seemed like the logical place to start her search for the Rowlands' file. She took a second to marvel at the clean efficiency of the space. Jessie didn't have a home office, just a small desk in her bedroom. She felt a pang of envy, but it passed quickly. Jessie loved being an assistant DA. She wouldn't trade it for anything.

Then you better hope Warren doesn't find out what you're doing.

The sound of a man clearing his throat behind her made her jump. She twisted around. As if summoned by her thoughts, Warren Williams stood in the doorway of Kelly's home office.

He wore a rumpled suit and looked even more beleaguered than usual. The dark circles under his eyes, and his waxy skin, suggested his new morning routine wasn't treating him well. "You want to tell me what the hell you think you're doing?"

Jessie straightened up. "Did you know the client files in Kelly's law office are missing?" Warren quirked an eyebrow, but remained quiet. "I came here to see if she had any files in her home. When I got here, there were two men—"

"I heard."

"They were looking for files, too. I'm sure of it. I'm just hoping they fled before they could find everything."

"The police believe the men were burglars."

"They weren't, Warren. They were looking for something. And they were careful not to make a mess. This was Douglas Shaw and Boffo Products Corporation, the defendants in Kelly's big lawsuit. You've got to see that."

Warren rubbed his tired-looking face. "No, actually. What I see is insubordination. I told you to stay away from this case. AID closed its investigation. The police department doesn't want you nosing around here. I already received one angry phone call and I don't plan to receive more. You are going to stop right now."

"I can't do that," Jessie said.

Warren's face darkened. "Why not?"

"Because I need her help," a voice said.

Warren spun around and Jessie stared past him. Noah Snyder strolled casually into Kelly's home office, a friendly smile on his face. "Hello, Warren. How are you doing? Finally get that hemorrhoid problem under control?"

Warren's face darkened another shade, and Jessie could see the internal struggle behind his eyes. "What are you doing here, Noah?" Warren said.

Jessie was as curious as Warren to know the answer. Snyder walked past Warren and stood at Jessie's side. He put a hand around her waist, a gesture that was either a show of solidarity, sexual harassment, or a little bit of both. Jessie tried not to cringe.

"What am I doing here?" Snyder said. "I'm working on the biggest case of my career. Major class-action lawsuit, in case you haven't heard. I'm going to bankrupt those toy-making mother-fuckers. Just as soon as Jessie gives me Kelly Lee's working file. Right, Jess?"

"Right," Jessie said, following his lead. "That's why we're both here. I'm helping Noah find the file so he can pick up the Rowlands' case. Professional courtesy. Nothing more."

"Okay with you, boss man?" Snyder said.

Warren rubbed his face again, seeming to consider. "Fine. Spend an hour—no more than that—and see if you can find the file. But that's it, Jessie. I mean it. There are only so many excuses I can make to my friends in the police department before they decide they're not my friends anymore. Do you understand?"

"Completely. Thank you."

"I'm going back to the office," Warren said. "Noah, nice seeing you again. And relatively sober, too. A pleasant surprise for everyone."

Jessie waited until Warren had left before turning her attention to Snyder. "You said you wanted nothing to do with this case. You left Kelly Lee's office without even saying goodbye. Did you grow a conscience?"

The silver-haired lawyer looked taken aback. "Conscience? Hell no. I have an associate who monitors the police band for me. She picked up on the home invasion here. I figured you might need me. When I got here and saw fat-ass reading you your rights, I decided to help you out."

Jessie couldn't help smiling. "I have news for you, Noah. That's called a conscience."

Snyder shook his head. "It's called a favor. I did you one, and now you owe me one. In fact, since the favor I did you was so gargantuan—I mean, I basically saved your job—I think you owe me *a few* favors in return. For starters, you're going to help me with this Rowland case."

"If Kelly Lee's file is here in the apartment, we'll find it."

Snyder smirked. "We both know the chances of finding that file are slim to none. I told you, I'm not putting in the work to handle this case from the ground up. If you can't find the file, then you'll need to do the work for me. Research the law, write the briefs, and prepare my talking points so I can get Judge Dax to certify the class or at least let us proceed alone on the claim. That's favor number one."

What had begun as a feeling of relief turned to a sinking feeling in her gut. "Okay. Fine. Substitute yourself as counsel and I'll do the heavy legal lifting for you. What's favor number two?"

"I'm not sure yet. But don't worry, Jess. I'm sure I'll think of something."

16

GRAHAM GRIPPED the steering wheel of her unmarked Ford Police Interceptor and tried to force away thoughts of what could have happened to Jessie. She knew it wasn't Jessie's fault she'd walked in on two men who'd broken into Kelly Lee's apartment, but she felt angry anyway. Jessie shouldn't have been there. She shouldn't be obsessing over Kelly Lee's death at all. Those men could have attacked her instead of running. Or worse.

She reached her destination, a complex of squat, nondescript buildings in a corporate park outside the city. The headquarters of Boffo Products Corporation.

Jessie believed Kelly Lee had been murdered, and that Douglas Shaw and his company were behind it. Graham wasn't convinced, but she had to admit to her own lack of objectivity. How could any cop be objective about a lawyer who'd brought a police misconduct claim against her? Plus, when she'd dropped in on Ross Reid at the gym to ask the detective about the accident investigation, he'd seemed evasive—even a little hostile. She had enough doubt in her own mind to create an unavoidable question.

That question was, *What if Jessie's right?*

It wouldn't be the first time. The woman made an irritating habit of it. Graham couldn't help but smile.

Her smile dropped when a familiar vehicle drove into the parking lot. The driver parked, opened the door, and got out. It was Mark Leary. Graham scrambled out of her own car as the man marched toward the building's entrance.

"Leary!"

He spun around and his eyes widened. "Emily?"

"What are you doing here?" she said.

"Getting to the bottom of this mess before Jessie gets herself fired," he said. "Or worse."

"She told you about what happened today at Lee's apartment?"

"I have my sources."

"So she didn't tell you?" Graham wasn't surprised. She knew Jessie chafed at Leary's sometimes over-protective attitude toward her. "Maybe that's something you should think about."

"I'm not about to take relationship advice from you." She felt the sting of his words. He must have seen her reaction in her face. "I'm sorry. I didn't mean that, Emily. I'm just upset."

"Whatever."

"Emily—"

"It's not worth talking about. What's your plan? You're just going to march in there and demand to speak to the CEO of the company?"

"Yeah." A look of uncertainty flashed across his face. "Usually works."

"With a badge."

"I'm a detective with the District's Attorney's Office." He stood up a little straighter.

"And I'm an actual homicide detective. I think we're more likely to get past his flunkies using my creds."

"The PPD investigation is closed. How are you going to explain this to your superiors?"

"How are you?" she shot back.

They stood for a second, staring at each other in the parking lot. A chilly fall breeze made Graham's jacket flap around her.

"Well, we're not going to learn anything by having a staring contest with each other," Leary said.

The statement was true, but she still held eye-contact until he looked away first.

"What was your game plan?" he said.

"Ask him about the lawsuit. Ask him about the accident. See if I can shake him up."

Leary nodded. "You're good at shaking people up." Hurriedly, he added, "I meant that one as a compliment."

"I know." She gave him a smile and he seemed to relax. "I always wondered what it would have been like to work with you in the Homicide Division. I guess this is pretty close."

"I'll try not to disappoint."

They walked to the building. Graham couldn't help staring at the expansive lobby. The plain exterior of the building had not hinted at the opulence within. A huge glass display case dominated the waiting area, featuring an array of toys. Artifacts from the company's history, she guessed. Apparently, Boffo was a successful venture.

There was a woman in a suit sitting on one of several couches. She glanced up at them as they entered, then returned her attention to her phone. Graham crossed the wide space and approached the receptionist.

"We're here to see Douglas Shaw."

The woman peered at her through stylish glasses. "Do you have an appointment?"

"Don't need one." Graham held up her badge.

"Is there someone else who could help you? Mr. Shaw is the

president and CEO of the company. His schedule is very busy—"

"I'm a detective with the Philadelphia Police Department, and my colleague here is with the District Attorney's Office. We're here to speak with Mr. Shaw."

"Give me a moment, please." She lifted a phone from her desk and touched a button, then turned her chair and conversed quietly with the person on the other end of the line. She put down the phone. "Mr. Shaw can make some time to see you."

"Thanks."

A man emerged from a doorway and approached the desk. He looked more like one of the toys in the display case than an actual human being—exaggeratedly brawny, like a bad knockoff of a He Man action figure, his body barely able to fit in the suit he'd stuffed himself into. He did not speak or introduce himself. He gestured for Graham and Leary to follow him.

Leary caught her eye, arched a brow. She moved her shoulders in a slight shrug.

The man led them toward a bank of elevators, then kept walking. Graham realized there was another elevator, set apart from the others, with a keypad instead of a call button. The man tapped a code into the keypad.

"My name's Mark Leary, by the way. And you are?"

The man stared at Leary. Leary stared back. Either the guy was mute, or he had the social etiquette of a recluse. *Or a thug,* she thought.

The elevator doors opened, revealing a spacious elevator car. The man gestured for them to step inside.

More silence as they rode to the top floor. There was a vein just under the shelf of the man's chin that pulsed rhythmically. Graham couldn't help staring at it. She'd dealt with meatheads like this guy before—lots of criminals liked to walk around with oversized goons—but something about this particular oversized guy intrigued her. Maybe it was the strangeness of seeing him in an otherwise typical corporate environment.

The elevator doors opened directly onto Douglas Shaw's office suite. The space was massive, the size of four or five normal offices put together. Three of the walls were floor-to-ceiling windows, with a view of a lake Graham hadn't noticed on her drive into the office park. Seated behind a large, glass desk was a gray-haired man who must be Douglas Shaw. He rose from his chair and came toward them. With a nod, he dismissed the big man. He extended a hand to Graham.

"I'm Douglas Shaw." His tone was clipped and aristocratic. She disliked him immediately.

"Emily Graham." They shook hands. Shaw's grip was firm. "This is Mark Leary."

"My receptionist did not tell me the purpose of your visit."

"She didn't know it."

"Is this about Kelly Lee's accident?" he said.

Graham and Leary exchanged a look. "Why would you assume that?" Leary said.

"I can't imagine any other reason you would be here. I heard about the accident."

"You don't sound too broken up about it," Graham said.

"I'm not, Detective Graham. And frankly, I'm too old to bother pretending. Kelly Lee was a bottom-feeding ambulance chaser. The world is better without her."

Graham's own thoughts about Lee's death had been almost exactly the same, but hearing Shaw speak them aloud made her recoil both from him and from herself. Shaw was cold, hard, indifferent. She didn't want to be like him.

"I gotta say," Leary said, "you're about as different as possible from what I'd imagine a toymaker to be."

"I'm not a toymaker. I'm a businessman."

Graham noticed that their musclebound escort had not

returned to the elevator. Instead, the big man stood erect against the wall, watching. Apparently, Shaw did not intend their meeting to be a long one.

"As a businessman, you must have been pretty concerned about the class-action lawsuit Ms. Lee was bringing against your company," Graham said.

"Technically, she was not bringing a class-action lawsuit. In order to do that, you need a court to certify the class under Pennsylvania law. She was in the *process* of seeking certification, which I understand the judge was going to deny."

The man's air of confidence surprised her. "How would you know that, if the judge hasn't ruled yet?"

"Call it intuition. Do you have any other questions, Detective?"

"Where were you on the night of the accident?"

Shaw let out a laugh. "I was attending a very nice fundraising event with a large group of people who would be happy to corroborate my attendance."

"Of course you were," Graham said. That meant nothing, of course. She'd never thought this sixty-five-year-old man had personally dirtied his hands tampering with Kelly Lee's car. He'd paid someone else to do it, assuming he was involved at all.

"I heard you tried to settle the case," Graham said. "If you were so sure you'd win, why offer to pay Lee and her clients?"

He shrugged. "That's how the system works. It's not about right or wrong. You settle to avoid litigation."

Graham knew this all too well. Her own police misconduct claim had been settled by the city, despite the claim being utterly meritless. As Shaw said, that was how the system worked.

Shaw seemed to be watching her expression closely. He turned away and sighed. "Detective, what happened to the Rowlands' son was tragic, but it was not caused by our toys. Our toys are safe. Had the case gone to trial, I have no doubt we would have prevailed. But I didn't want to go to trial. I didn't want the bad publicity that would have come with a public trial, and I didn't want the expense of hiring lawyers, experts, and the myriad other costs of litigation. That is why I was pushing for a settlement."

"But they rejected the offer," Leary pointed out.

"Yes. I believe we still would have won in court. Now, I guess we'll never know."

"I think you will know," Graham said. "The Rowlands have a new lawyer."

Shaw leaned forward. "Are you certain? I wasn't notified."

Graham didn't like the look that came across his face. It was angry, almost predatory.

Shaw gestured to the musclebound man. "I have a meeting, so we're going to have to stop. I would be happy to respond to any follow-up questions by email."

Shaw extended his hand again. Graham did not take it. Neither did Leary.

"One more question," Graham said. "Kelly Lee's office seems to be missing a lot of files, including the Rowland file. Just before I drove over here, two men were witnessed breaking into her apartment and searching for something. Do you know anything about that?"

Something flashed in Shaw's eyes. Anger, definitely, but she also thought she saw genuine surprise. Maybe he really wasn't involved. Or maybe the two goons hadn't told him they'd been caught in the act. "Why would I know anything about that?" He turned to the big man, who was still standing against the wall. "Troy, please show our guests out."

Shaw turned away. The big man—Troy—advanced toward Graham and Leary. His huge frame seemed to fill her entire field of vision.

She sensed Leary stiffening beside her, and her own body tensed. Instinctively, she knew a time might come when she'd have to fight this giant, but now was not the time. She and Leary walked with Troy to the elevator. All the way, Graham felt the stare of Douglas Shaw at her back.

17

As she continued her search of Kelly Lee's apartment, Jessie tried not to think about the favors she now owed Snyder. She would have plenty of time to regret that devil's bargain later, she supposed. For now, the priority was finding anything Kelly might have left in her apartment that could either help Snyder with the Rowland case, provide evidence that the accident Kelly had died in had been a murder, or, ideally, both.

"This is a waste of time." Snyder leaned against the wall. Jessie had searched Kelly's home office and found nothing. Instead of actually helping her, Snyder seemed content to watch and complain. The only searching he'd done was to look for a liquor cabinet, which he had been gravely disappointed not to find.

"Let's at least check the bedroom before we give up."

"The bedroom?" Snyder quirked an eyebrow. "Now we're talking."

"Don't get excited. I meant check for the Rowland file." Thinking of her own experience, Jessie knew that sometimes she liked to pull her laptop into bed. Maybe Kelly had similar habits.

"Hey, why not?" Snyder said. "It's only my whole day we're wasting here."

In the bedroom, Jessie found more potential places where Kelly might store a file. There was another bookcase, two nightstands with drawers, a big dresser, and a wardrobe. Jessie started looking through the furniture. Finally, in the nightstand to the left of the bed, she found a folder in the drawer. When Jessie pulled it out and opened it, she found notes written on yellow legal paper. Legal terms covered the pages.

"I think I found something."

She skimmed the pages of neat handwriting, but her enthusiasm lessened with each page. There were no references to Deanna or Ken Rowland, their son, Boffo, or even class action lawsuits in general. The notes seemed to be about other cases Kelly had been working on. Jessie saw names she didn't recognize, insurance companies, phone numbers. She saw references to accident reports, insurance claims, and doctors. Jessie assumed the doctors were either experts that helped Kelly assess claims, or defendants in medical malpractice cases.

She reached the last page of the file and a name caught her attention. She stared more closely at the page in case she'd misread Kelly's handwriting. But there was no mistaking what she'd printed there: *Victoria Briscoe, University of Pennsylvania Hospital.*

"Judging by the look on your face, I take it you found something useful?" Snyder said. He crossed the room to stand at her side. He squinted at the sheet of paper, then shot her a questioning look. "This has to do with the Rowlands?"

"No. I mean, I don't think so. But I know the name Vicki Briscoe."

"Is she hot?"

Jessie ignored him. *Could she be the same Vicki Briscoe?* Had to be. How many doctors in Philadelphia had that name? Jessie read further and learned that Briscoe had been the subject of a medical malpractice claim. From what Jessie could gather from Kelly's notes, the case had settled. The hospital's insurance company made a payment to Kelly's client—Briscoe's patient— and the hospital fired Briscoe. There was even a note indicating that Briscoe might be stripped of her medical license.

Jessie realized she was holding her breath. She let it out and forced herself to breathe.

"I don't get it," Snyder said. "If this Briscoe woman's case isn't related to the Rowlands, why are you staring at it?"

Jessie stepped away from Snyder, trying to block out the sound of his talking so she could think. This new information— that Kelly Lee had pursued a medical malpractice claim against Vicki Briscoe that had resulted in the loss of Briscoe's job and possibly her medical license—changed everything.

She pulled out her phone and called Emily Graham.

———

THIRTY MINUTES LATER, Jessie entered the Chestnut Street Diner in Center City and found the booth where Emily Graham waited with another woman. "Hey."

Graham smiled, but it looked forced. Jessie felt the weight of the tension between them and had to shake off a feeling of sadness. She forced herself not to think about it. They were good friends who'd had a disagreement, and they would get past it. For now, what mattered was that Graham had set up this meeting on short notice, and Jessie needed to stay focused.

"Jessie Black, meet Lorena Torres," Graham said.

Torres rose and shook Jessie's hand. Jessie knew she was a detective in the PPD's Organized Crime Unit. She was a slim, attractive Latina, with a firm grip and a direct stare. "Nice to finally meet you," Torres said.

Jessie smiled awkwardly. *Finally* meet her? She wasn't sure what that meant, but she nodded and sat down across the table from the detective. "I appreciate you making the time on such short notice."

"Well, I couldn't pass up an opportunity to meet the great Jessica Black," Torres said.

Jessie shifted in her seat, unsure how to respond to the woman's sarcastic tone.

Graham cleared her throat. "This is kind of awkward, but you're both my friends, so let's get everything out in the open. Jessie, when Lorena was a rookie cop, she came up the ranks with Mark Leary. They had kind of an on-again, off-again thing."

"Mostly off again," Torres said with a self-deprecating smile. "He was never that into me. I guess I wasn't his type." She seemed to study Jessie, as if trying to determine what Leary's type was.

Jessie tried not to feel uncomfortable, but it was pretty hard. "I... I'm not really sure what to say."

Torres laughed and lifted her left hand. A wedding ring caught the light. "No worries. Happily married now. I've just always been curious about you."

The tension dissipated, and Jessie let out a breath of relief. A waitress appeared with plates of food and placed pancakes in front of Torres and a salad in front of Graham. "Sorry," Graham said. "We didn't know how long you would be, so we ordered without you. Do you want anything?"

"Just coffee, please," Jessie said to the waitress.

The Chestnut Street Diner was a popular destination for cops because the owner always served members of the police force free of charge. Whatever income he lost in free eggs and Taylor Ham, he more than made up for with a seemingly endless streak of zero crime. Jessie was not the biggest fan of the cuisine, but she wasn't really in a position to argue.

When the waitress left their table, Torres ate a bite of pancake. "Emily said you're looking for information on the Briscoe family?"

"That's right," Jessie said. "Vicki Briscoe in particular. Has she or her family been the subject of any Organized Crime investigations recently?"

"This has something to do with a murder case the DA's Office is working on?" Torres said.

"Any information you can give me would be helpful." Jessie sensed, by the way Graham's posture stiffened, that her friend didn't appreciate her dodging the question. Torres didn't seem to notice.

"I can tell you that Vicki Briscoe is bad news. You probably know that her father Ray is the head of a motorcycle gang called the Dark Hounds. They're into all kinds of bad business. Drugs. Human trafficking. They operate out of a farm in Lancaster that Ray swindled from some Amish family years ago."

"Is Vicki involved in her father's gang?" Jessie said.

"I don't think she's an official member of the Dark Hounds Motorcycle Club, but she grew up in that environment, that culture. We've heard that she went to medical school to get out of the family business, but...." Torres trailed off.

The waitress brought Jessie's coffee. She took one sip, struggled not to make a face, and put it down. "But what?"

"Word is she lost her medical license," Torres said. "I don't know the whole story. She broke some rules in the operating room. Violated the ethics of her profession."

"Do you know what she's been up to since losing her license?"

Torres ate some more of her pancakes, then wiped her mouth on a napkin. "Nothing has come up. We try to keep her father's operation under surveillance, obviously, but there are limits. She's been seen with her father a lot, but there's nothing too unusual about that. We haven't seen her do anything against the law. But it's probably only a matter of time."

"Thanks again for meeting with me," Jessie said. "This has been really helpful."

"Can you tell me how it relates to your murder case?"

Jessie hesitated. "I really can't talk about it yet. I'm sorry."

A look of annoyance flashed across Torres's face. Jessie wasn't surprised. Torres had shared information, and Jessie wasn't reciprocating. That was the kind of thing that pissed detectives off, and as "the kind of woman who was Leary's type," Jessie had already started off the conversation on shaky footing. "Look, when I'm a little further along, I'll fill you in."

"Does this have to do with the missing councilwoman in Lancaster? We suspect Ray Briscoe is behind her disappearance, but we haven't found any evidence yet."

"Missing councilwoman?" Jessie said.

"If this is related, you better loop me in."

Jessie sipped the awful coffee again, just to delay answering. "You'll be the first to know if anything develops."

Torres nodded slowly, then returned to her food.

To be polite, Jessie remained at the table while the other two women finished their lunch. When the waitress told them their meal was on the house, Graham left a tip and the three of them walked outside. Torres said goodbye, got in an unmarked car, and drove away. Jessie was about to hit the sidewalk when Graham touched her arm.

"Sorry. I didn't realize how awkward that would be. But you said you needed to talk to someone in Organized Crime, and Lorena's the best."

"It's fine. You helped me out. Thank you. I appreciate it, especially with ... you know—"

"With you dedicating every second to avenging the woman who accused me of abusing my power as an officer of the law?"

Jessie nodded. "Yeah."

"Well, I'm still pissed off about that, but I'm working through it. Where are you headed? I'll give you a ride. There are some things I need to tell you."

"Can you give me a ride to the garage where I keep my car?"

Graham's eyes narrowed with concern. "You're driving somewhere?"

Jessie knew better than to try to conceal her plans from Emily Graham. "I'll explain in the car."

18

IN GRAHAM'S UNMARKED FORD, heading toward the garage where Jessie kept her car, Graham said, "I assume the questions you were asking about Vicki Briscoe have something to do with Kelly Lee?"

Jessie stared out the windshield at Philadelphia traffic. "Do you really want to know?"

"I'm asking, aren't I?"

"I thought you didn't want anything to do with looking into Kelly's accident."

Jessie saw her friend's jaw flex. "I never said that."

"Okay. I guess I misinterpreted."

Graham piloted the car through a snarl of traffic, then seemed to relax slightly. "I'm a good detective, regardless of what someone like Kelly Lee might claim."

"I agree. I would never believe otherwise."

Graham nodded. "I gave Douglas Shaw an unexpected visit."

"What?" Jessie leaned forward. The seat belt cut into her shoulder.

"We had a little talk about the case against Boffo, and about Lee's convenient death."

"Just you and Shaw? No other cops?"

Graham seemed to hesitate. "No other cops, but...." She took her eyes off the road and glanced at Jessie. "I ran into Leary in the parking lot. We interviewed Shaw together."

"Leary was there?" Leary had insisted that she stay away from the case, but then he'd secretly gone to investigate it himself? She knew his motive had probably been to protect her, but she felt a rush of anger in spite of that—or maybe because of that. She was an assistant DA, not some naive girl in need of protection.

"He's trying to look out for you," Graham said. "So am I."

"Thanks so much," she said sarcastically. "Did you happen to learn anything useful while you were protecting me from myself?"

"Not really. Shaw isn't sad about Lee's death. He admitted that. But that's all he admitted."

"What about the missing files? The men I caught searching Kelly's apartment?"

"I confronted him about that. If anything, he seemed kind of surprised."

Jessie thought about that. She pushed her anger down and said, "What was your gut reaction?"

Graham let out a breath and shook her head. "I'm not sure. It's definitely possible that he was involved in Lee's death and the theft of her files, but I didn't get the strong feeling that I was talking to a liar. Or a killer."

"What about Leary?"

"You'd have to ask him, I guess."

"I plan to." She felt her anger return.

"Your turn. Why am I driving you to your car? You only use it when you leave the city."

"I need to run something down. A loose end."

"Related to Vicki Briscoe?" Concern filled Graham's face.

"Jessie, the Briscoes are dangerous people. You cannot start poking around in their lives, or anyone else in that gang."

"You heard Torres say Vicki Briscoe lost her medical license recently, right?"

Graham nodded as she swerved around a car that was parallel parking. "Yes."

"Who do you think brought the medical malpractice claim?"

Graham let out a low whistle. "So now you have two suspects in a murder the official police report says didn't happen?"

"Relax, Emily. I'm not going to put myself in danger. I know someone who knows Vicki Briscoe. I'm just going to visit him, get a sense of whether she might have been involved. If I think she was, I'll let you know and hopefully the PPD can run with it instead of me."

Graham glanced at her with a skeptical look. "And who is this person?"

Jessie leaned back in her seat. They were in stop and go traffic now, and someone a few cars behind was leaning on the horn. "Several years ago, I tried a felony-murder case against a man named Trevor Galway. He and his friends robbed a liquor store, armed with shotguns. It would have been a straightforward robbery except that some kid in the back of the store had his own gun and tried to be a hero. One of Galway's buddies blew the guy's head off. Under the felony-murder rule, all of them were guilty."

"So Galway went down on a murder charge?"

"Yes. And when we looked into him, we learned that his girlfriend was the daughter of a well-known area criminal, Ray Briscoe. But we didn't find any connection between Briscoe's gang and the robbery-murder."

"His girlfriend was Vicki Briscoe?"

Jessie nodded. "I thought the defense might call her to the stand as a character witness either during the defense stage of

Galway's trial or afterward during the sentencing phase. But she never even came close to the courthouse. She dropped the guy entirely."

"Cold."

"Exactly. That's why I think Galway might be willing to share some information about his former girlfriend with me now."

"It's an idea," Graham said, still looking skeptical. "Assuming he doesn't hate you more than he hates her. For, you know, being the person who actually put him in prison."

Jessie conceded the point with a nod. "There's that. Still worth a try."

"Where is he?"

"Frackville."

Graham made a face.

"I've been there before," Jessie said.

State Correctional Institution–Frackville was a prison complex off Interstate 81 in Schuylkill County. Getting there would take Jessie about two hours driving through mostly rural areas—four hours round trip—and when she arrived, she'd be entering one of Pennsylvania's toughest maximum-security correctional facilities.

"Frackville is dungeon for monsters," Graham said.

"I'll have the protection of guards at all times. And Galway's not so much a monster as a victim of his own bad decisions. He's not a member of the Dark Hounds, or any other gang."

"Promise me you'll be as careful as possible."

"Come on, Emily. You know me."

"That's what worries me." She pulled off the street, and into the parking garage.

19

AFTER A TWO-HOUR DRIVE, Jessie turned her car onto the grounds of the Frackville State Correctional Institution. Its six housing units were spread over about thirty-five acres of land, set off from the surrounding towns by a buffer of about 174 acres. From the comfort of her car, the area seemed serene, peaceful. If not for the razor wire and the guard towers, it might have resembled a college campus. But she knew that illusion would burst the moment she stepped foot inside.

The place was, as Graham had described it, a dungeon full of monsters. A maximum security prison housing over a thousand of the state's most violent adult male inmates.

She parked her car, took a deep breath, and opened the door. Inside, she waited while guards confirmed her ID, then escorted her past several doors, gates, and barricades to a visitation room. Here she waited while other guards retrieved Trevor Galway from his housing unit.

The visitation room was a fifteen-foot-square box with cement walls. Metal furniture was bolted to the floor. A table and two chairs, cold to the touch. She resisted the instinct to shiver or hug herself. She knew she was probably being observed, and it was hard enough to be taken seriously as a woman in this place.

Through the cement walls she could hear the typical sounds she'd come to associate with prisons and jails—echoing footsteps, distant yelling, the loud buzz of doors opening and closing. It was a grim atmosphere.

A louder buzz sounded as the door to the visitation room unlocked and opened. A burly corrections officer delivered Trevor Galway to the room. The lanky, red-haired inmate glanced briefly at her, then fixed his gaze down at his white, prison-issued slippers. Jessie watched silently as the guard went through the ritual of securing Galway to the floor and the table by threading his handcuff and ankle chains through rings attached to both surfaces. The jingling sound was like a dark parody of a happy Christmas scene. When the procedure was finished, and Galway was secured, the guard finally took his attention off the inmate and looked at Jessie.

"Just knock on the door when you're done." With that, he exited the room, leaving Jessie alone with a man she had prosecuted and convicted of murder.

An odor of sweat and musk wafted off the man. He had been in his late twenties when Jessie prosecuted his felony-murder trial. Now, in his early thirties, he was still a relatively young man. But he didn't look it. Prison had hardened him, taken the youthful vitality out of him. He looked almost like a different person.

"Thanks for agreeing to meet with me, Trevor," she said, straining to keep her voice level.

Galway looked at her. She was surprised by the lack of resentment or anger in his gaze. She'd expected hostility, but, if anything, he looked happy to see her. Or maybe just happy to have any visitor. "Sure. Sure." He leaned toward her eagerly. His chains jingled. "You said you wanted my help with some kind of case? Does that mean you can help me, too? We can make some kind of deal?"

The look of hope in his face gave her a pang of guilt. She wasn't here with authorization to make any deals. Hell, she wasn't here with any authorization at all. "It's too early to talk about deals. Right now, I'm just curious if you have some information that might be helpful."

"Sure. Sure," he said again, nodding his head. The phrase seemed to be a kind of verbal tic, but she didn't remember him having it during his trial. Had he picked it up during his incarceration? Jessie pretended not to notice.

"I'd like to talk to you about the Dark Hounds Motorcycle Club."

"Don't know what I can tell you about them. I was never a member, you know. I mean, I met Ray a bunch because of Vicki, and I guess I saw some stuff, but I wasn't in the club."

"I understand that, Trevor."

"I think about killing myself every day, you know?"

The non-sequitur threw her for a second. She took a breath, studying him. "I'm sure it's very difficult for you in here."

"Sure. Sure. But that's not what I mean. This place"—he waved a hand—"it's not that bad. But the dead guy—you know, the man Billy shot—every time I try to sleep, I see that guy. It was like, one second he's a human being like you or me just going through his day. Just doing his job at the store. And then Billy moves his finger." Galway demonstrated by lifting his shackled wrist from the table and twitching the index finger of his right hand. "Just this little movement of his finger. And the guy's dead. Gone."

Jessie felt an ache of sympathy for the man. It was a quirk of the felony-murder rule that people who didn't actively commit a murder, and may have never murdered anyone in their lives, could still be convicted of murder simply by being an accomplice to a crime in which a person died. One of the purposes of the rule was to serve as a deterrent to people to engage in potentially violent crimes. Jessie had mixed feelings about it, but overall, she supported the idea, even as she felt bad for men like Galway.

"That man's death was a terrible tragedy," Jessie said.

Galway nodded miserably. "Sure. Sure."

"I'm actually here to talk about Vicki Briscoe. At the time of your arrest, I understand you had been together for several years, were even living together I believe?"

"Right."

"I'm hoping you can give me some insight into her character. I know about her father's record, obviously, but I also know being a criminal isn't genetic. Can you tell me if you think Vicki is capable of killing someone out of spite, or for revenge?"

He looked away from her. "I don't want to talk about Vicki."

"Why not?"

"I just don't."

"Do you still have feelings for her?" Jessie had not expected that to be the case. "You know Vicki could have testified on your behalf at your trial, right? She could have made a real difference, especially at your sentencing hearing. Did your defense attorney tell you that?"

His gaze roamed the bare walls of the room as he avoided her gaze.

"Trevor, listen to me. Vicki could have told the court about your good character. The judge might not have stuck you in this place for so many years."

Galway shrugged. "I don't know about that."

"Has she visited you here?"

"It's a long ride."

"It's two hours. I did it."

He shrugged again.

"Trevor," she pressed, "Vicki has no right to expect loyalty from you. She abandoned you."

Galway surprised her again, this time by letting out a rueful laugh. "I doubt Vick expects anything. She's probably forgotten about me. Sure, sure. That's for the best. But I love her. Always will."

"Okay." Jessie took another breath. She'd banked on Galway's resentment, but that wasn't going to work. She needed to take a different tack. "Those are your feelings. I respect that. But can you tell me anything? Anything about Vicki's involvement in her father's motorcycle club? Anything about her plans for the future? I know she went to medical school and became a doctor. That must have been important to her. Not an easy road. Can you tell me about that?"

"I told you I don't want to talk about Vicki."

Jessie suppressed a sigh. She'd traveled a long way to come to this prison. The thought of turning around for another two-hour drive, after learning nothing, was dispiriting. "Can you tell me if Vicki knew anything about explosives? For example, could she arrange for a car to explode, and make it look like an accident?"

She saw the muscles bunch beneath his lean face. He looked away from her.

"Trevor?" She leaned toward him. "Trevor, you said Gustavo Martìnez's death still haunts you." Her use of the name of the man who died in the convenience store brought his gaze back to hers. "There's a death that haunts *me* right now. A woman I used to know. A friend. I'm trying to figure out what happened to her. Please help me with this. I need to know if Vicki, or anyone she's close with, has expertise in explosives."

With startling suddenness, Galway's face filled with rage. "Stay away from Vicki or you'll be sorry!"

"Why does that question upset you?"

"I want you to leave." Galway twisted away from her. She could see his expression soften as he regained control of himself. "I'm not talking to you anymore. Not another word."

Jessie stood up, crossed to the door, and knocked for the corrections officer. She wasn't going to get any more cooperation from Galway, but maybe she wasn't going to leave as empty-handed as she'd feared. The way he'd reacted to her question about explosives meant something. If he'd responded with a denial, or surprise, or even silence, she might have taken nothing from it. But his sudden, unprovoked anger? That could only mean Jessie was on to something.

20

By the time Jessie finished the long drive back from the Frackville State Correctional Institution, returned her car to its parking garage, and walked back to her apartment building, she was exhausted. She unlocked her door and practically staggered inside. The lights were off, which she was not expecting.

"Leary?" She dropped her bag and keys on the kitchenette counter. "Okay, guess I'm alone."

"Not quite," said a voice from the shadows of the living room.

Jessie swung around. At the same moment, the light went on. A woman sat on her couch. Red hair, angry face, serious-looking boots. Vicki Briscoe.

Jessie advanced toward her. "What the hell do you think you're doing here? You broke into my apartment?"

Briscoe shrugged. She looked totally relaxed, reclining on the couch with one leg crossed over the other, as casual as a visiting friend. A cold feeling of uncertainty spread through Jessie's body. How dangerous was this woman? Somehow the lack of an aggressive stance made her seem even more unnerving.

"I hear you've been asking questions about me," Briscoe said.

Don't let her intimidate you. "Isn't that an occupational hazard in your line of business?"

"The medical business?"

"The organized crime business."

Briscoe studied her evenly. "I've been doing some research on you, too, Jessica Black. Actually, my file on you dates back years. All the way back to when you sent Trevor away for a murder he had nothing to do with."

"He was an accomplice to a crime during which—"

"I'm familiar with the felony-murder rule."

"I imagine you're familiar with a lot of laws. Criminal ones and maybe civil ones, too. For example, the kind that might be applicable to a medical malpractice case."

A half-smile twisted Briscoe's face, but it seemed to hint at barely concealed rage rather than amusement. "Is that what you're interested in? My med-mal case?"

"I'm interested in you leaving. Now."

"Or what? You'll call the police?"

"I'm calling the police either way."

Briscoe sat still for a moment. Jessie pressed her lips together, hoping her expression wasn't betraying her rapidly beating heart. Briscoe rose gracefully from the couch. She headed for the door, which was behind Jessie. Jessie stiffened as the woman came even with her. Briscoe gave off a dangerous vibe, like a jungle cat—beautiful and graceful, but also unpredictable and deadly. Briscoe must have noticed the tensing of Jessie's muscles. She smirked and met Jessie's eyes. "You're scared."

"You're the one who broke into the home of an assistant district attorney. You should be scared."

"That sounds almost like a threat."

"Take it how you will."

With shocking speed, Briscoe pivoted, grabbed one of Jessie's wrists, and twisted her arm behind her back. Pain raced up her arm. She struggled, but Briscoe's grip was too strong. The woman jerked her arm upward as far as Jessie's muscles and bones would allow. Agony made her vision blur. Her suit jacket split with the sound of tearing fabric. She gritted her teeth, waiting for the explosion of breaking bones.

Then the pressure eased and she felt Briscoe's breath at her ear. "You want to trade threats, I'll give you a real one. If I ever find out you're talking to people about me again—family, ex-boyfriend, *anyone*—I will come back here. You won't see me coming. I'll break this arm and both of your legs, too. And that will just be the warmup."

Briscoe let go. Jessie tumbled forward, banging her legs against the coffee table and falling to the floor. She clutched her arm, massaging the muscles. Her gaze locked on the woman looming above her. She braced for another attack—for a second, Briscoe looked angry enough. But then the woman took a breath, straightened her hair, and seemed to regain her composure.

Even though Jessie's survival instinct told her to stay on the floor, not say a word, and let the woman leave, the burn of her indignation was too powerful. "You have a temper." She knew there were tears in her eyes, but didn't care. "Did Kelly Lee make you angry, too? Did you blow up her car, make it look like an accident?"

Jessie closed her eyes, bracing herself for a kick or a punch. None came. When she opened her eyes, Briscoe was looking down at her with a thoughtful expression. "I had nothing to do with that accident."

"If I find out you did...."

"More threats from the woman curled up on the floor." Briscoe let out a musical laugh that might have been charming under different circumstances. "If any bitch had it coming, it was that scumbag lawyer. She cost me everything. And for what? A lousy insurance payout for her deadbeat client and her low-rent law practice? But I didn't kill her."

"You didn't want revenge?"

"Hell yeah, I wanted it. Lee ruined my life. She took away my dream. All my years of work. My accomplishments. My avocation. Everything. She left me with no choice but to crawl back to my father and his business, when all I ever wanted was to do my own thing in the real world. The legitimate world. So, did I think about exacting a little revenge? You bet I did. But I wouldn't have blown her up. I would've gotten my hands dirty. I would've strapped her to a chair, and gone to work on her with a dull knife. I would've made it last days. I would've carved her up and emptied her out. There wouldn't have been a nerve in her body that I didn't trace with the edge of a scalpel. I would have brought every bit of my medical knowledge to the project. Her car accident robbed me of that opportunity." Briscoe shrugged. "Lucky for her."

"Your bedside manner must have been one of your strongest assets as a doctor."

"I'm a surgeon. Bedside manner is optional."

"Before the accident, Kelly told me she felt like someone was following her. Was it you? Planning your torture session?"

Briscoe seemed to hesitate. Then she must have figured there was no harm in the confession. "I followed her. Didn't have much else to do without a job or a medical license."

"You stalked her."

"Are you going to prosecute me for stalking her now that she's dead? Is that a good use of the city's resources?"

"Maybe."

Briscoe smirked. "I doubt it."

"You terrorized her. You might not have gotten around to physically torturing her, but by following her, you caused her mental distress. Maybe she was distracted by that when she was driving. Maybe that's why she got into the car accident. If I can connect those dots, maybe I have a murder case against you."

Briscoe's face lost some of its smugness. "That sounds like a bullshit case."

"That's what lawyers like me do, right?" Jessie rose to her full height, even though moving her body hurt. She met Briscoe's gaze and didn't look away. "I put Trevor away for murder. He didn't pull a trigger, either. What makes you so sure I can't make a case against you?"

Briscoe stared at her for a long moment. "You're tougher than you seem. I'm impressed—a little bit. But don't push your luck with me."

Briscoe turned, opened the door, and left the apartment. Jessie waited until she heard the sound of the woman's footfalls in the hallway outside. Then she dropped onto the couch, put her head in her hands, and let out a shuddering breath.

21

LEARY CALLED. He was on his way home and wanted to know if she was in the mood for Chinese. After Vicki Briscoe's surprise visit, eating was the last thing on Jessie's mind, but she said yes. At least it would give her a few extra minutes to collect herself before he arrived.

Later, they ate dinner on the couch. The Chinese food was probably delicious. Jessie forced herself to eat, but could barely taste it. Her stomach churned and her hands were shaking. Could Leary tell? They were sitting on the same couch on which Vicki Briscoe had sat waiting for her in the darkness just hours ago. Right here on this couch, in this room, in her home.

There was a lot she wanted to talk to Leary about. She wanted to tell him about Briscoe. She wanted to ask him about his visit to Douglas Shaw's office and why he hid it from her. But she didn't trust herself to raise either of those topics right now, so she focused on chewing her General Tso's chicken.

"Is something wrong?" he said.

She shook her head, eating.

He put aside his own food. "You seem ... distant."

She shrugged. "I'm just thinking about work." Her usual, go-to excuse.

"Work, or Kelly Lee?" He sighed. "Emily told me you're still trying to get the police to investigate the accident. I told you that's a bad idea, Jessie. The PPD and the DA's Office—"

"When did Emily tell you? When the two of you questioned Douglas Shaw?"

Leary froze. "She told you about that?"

"Yeah. So I guess it's okay for you to disregard Warren's orders, but not me."

"I'm trying to protect you."

"You're trying to investigate, because you know I'm right. There's more to Kelly's accident than the police are willing to consider."

Leary sighed. "I don't know. Shaw didn't strike me as a guilty man trying to hide something."

"Who else would steal Kelly's files?"

He spread his hands. "How many people did she sue?"

"Point taken." Jessie got up. "Do you want a fortune cookie?"

"Sure." She handed him one, took one herself, and sat down next to him on the couch. He said, "Jessie, is everything okay? I mean, other than me acting like a hypocrite by doing what I told you not to do?"

"Yeah." She tried to laugh, but couldn't. *She* was the hypocrite, hiding much more from him than he'd hid from her. But she knew if she told him about Briscoe, he would become even more protective of her. She didn't need that from him right now. Didn't want it.

Her arm still ached from Briscoe's attack. Poking around the woman's life had been a mistake. Visiting Trevor Galway in prison, meeting with Lorena Torres of Organized Crime. Jessie should have known that these actions might get back to Briscoe, and that Briscoe would not be happy.

"*You will find treasure in an unexpected place*," Leary said, reading the slip of paper from his cookie. "What's yours say?"

She forced a smile and cracked open her fortune cookie. There was no slip of paper. Jessie made a face. "When I was a kid, my friends and I used to joke that if your fortune cookie was empty, you were going to die."

"Don't eat the cookie, then. If you don't eat the cookie, the fortune doesn't come true."

Jessie scoffed, but she didn't eat the cookie. "I'll clean up. You get changed."

She waited for Leary to disappear into the bedroom. She could hear him hanging his suit in the closet. She went into the bathroom, locked the door, and turned on the shower. The sound of pounding water filled the small room.

She took out her phone and called Graham. "It sounds like you're in a rain forest," Graham said.

"Bathroom. I'm running the shower for cover."

"Uh-oh."

"I can't talk to Leary about this, but I need to talk to someone. My heart is still racing."

"What is it?"

Jessie watched the mirror fog with steam. "Vicki Briscoe found out I was asking questions about her. She came to my home, threatened me."

"Are you okay?"

"Yeah." Jessie massaged her arm. It still ached.

"Did she hurt you?"

Jessie hesitated. "A little. Only to make a point."

"For God's sake, Jessie."

"She just wanted to make sure I know what a badass she is."

"Are you going to tell the police?"

"Other than you? No. I don't think that's the right move."

"Why not?"

"I don't think she had any involvement in Kelly Lee's accident. She admitted that she had been stalking Kelly, and that she had fantasized about getting some kind of revenge against her. I don't think she would have admitted those things if she caused the accident."

"So what? She broke into your apartment and assaulted you."

"She was angry that I visited her ex-boyfriend. The best thing to do is back off. I don't need anything from her, now that I'm pretty sure she's not the killer we're looking for. We'll go our separate ways. I'm sure one day, her time will come. I'll leave that to Lorena Torres and the Organized Crime Unit."

There was a stretch of silence on the line, with only the steady white noise of the shower. "If she comes back—if she so much as passes you on the street—you let me know, Jessie."

"I will."

"Promise."

"Yes. I promise."

22

WITH NOAH SNYDER officially substituted as plaintiffs' counsel in the case of *Rowland v. Boffo Products Corporation*, Judge Dax had authorized Snyder to obtain the sealed court files, which included all pleadings filed to date. While technically those documents were confidential, Snyder had ignored the court's order and immediately sent them to Jessie.

Now, sitting in her office, she stared through bleary eyes at the documents. Because the trial had been interrupted in its early stages, there wasn't much here—the complaint, answer, and reply, and the two motions Judge Dax had told her were currently pending before the court—the plaintiffs' motion to certify a class and the defense's motion for summary judgment. She found Kelly's brief in support of the motion to certify a class, and Boffo's brief in opposition. Typically, a reply brief— the movant's opportunity to address the arguments in the opposition brief—would complete the series, but there was no reply brief. Kelly's accident must have happened before she could file one.

The motion for summary judgment had a brief in support

by Boffo, a brief in opposition by Kelly, and a reply brief by Boffo.

Jessie called Snyder, on the off-chance that he'd missed sending her a document. "I don't see a reply brief for the motion to certify a class."

"Maybe Lee didn't bother with one?" Snyder suggested. "Reply briefs are optional."

"Kelly doesn't strike me as the kind of lawyer to take a short-cut. I think she may have died before she could file a reply."

"I guess that means we'll have to write one. And when I say *we*, I mean *you*."

"Yeah, I got that," she said, but Snyder had already disconnected. *Great.*

She'd work on a reply brief after she got her arms around the facts and the law. The problem was, the documents she had did not include a lot of information. Probably, Kelly had been holding back, not wanting to give the defense too much advance warning of her legal arguments and factual evidence she planned to use at trial. Also not in the file were the witnesses Kelly planned to call. These would have been produced during the discovery phase of the trial, which had not occurred yet.

All of that information was presumably in Kelly's own case file—the one that had vanished from her office along with her other client files.

Jessie stared at the documents she did have, unsure where to even start. The most immediate threats were the two motions currently pending before the court—the plaintiff's motion to certify as a class, and the defendant's motion for a summary judgment dismissing the case. Jessie needed to draft a reply brief, and then help Snyder prepare for a hearing. It was going to take a lot of research into areas of the law Jessie was not familiar with, along with an unhealthy amount of coffee, to even get started.

She felt a spark of hope when the phone on her desk rang. Maybe it was Snyder, calling to tell her he'd been joking about her doing all the work. But it wasn't Snyder. It was Warren. She picked up, said, "Hey."

"Come to my office."

"Everything okay?" His voice sounded tight, clipped, but she couldn't be sure that wasn't an effect of his new rising-before-the-dawn morning routine.

"Now, Jessie." *Not a good sign.*

Was he still angry that she'd gone to Kelly Lee's apartment? She thought she'd gotten him past that when she'd explained she was just helping Snyder. Walking to his office, she wondered what new thing might have irritated him. Had he somehow found out that Snyder had sent her the pleadings?

His office door was closed. *Definitely not a good sign.*

She knocked, took the half-snarl, half-grunt she heard through the door as an invitation, and went inside.

The small office was unusually crowded. Warren slouched in his office chair. Standing rigidly behind him was a man in a pristinely pressed police uniform whom she recognized as Captain Henderson, the head of the PPD Homicide Division. In the visitor chairs facing the desk were two people Jessie could recognize even just seeing the backs of their heads. Mark Leary and Emily Graham. They glanced back at her as she closed the door.

"Well, now we're all here," Warren said.

Jessie shifted her weight from one leg to the other. Nervousness burned through her. "What's going on?"

"I told you," Leary said quickly, before anyone else could respond. "Jessie doesn't know anything about this. We did it on our own. We didn't even tell her."

Graham remained silent, but glanced at Jessie with an apologetic look.

"What didn't you tell me?" Jessie said.

"Apparently, Douglas Shaw, the president and CEO of the company Kelly Lee was suing, received a visit from Detectives Graham and Leary, who claimed to be there as representatives of the PPD and the DA's Office," Warren said. "You can probably imagine the consequences when that happens to a wealthy, powerful person like Shaw."

"Angry complaints," Henderson put in. "Threats. Political pressure."

"You two had no authority to question Shaw," Warren said. "Your insubordination has put us in a very uncomfortable position."

"Insubordination?" Graham's voice rose. She looked to Henderson. "Captain, I—"

"AID closed the case," Henderson snapped. "The Homicide Division was not supposed to get involved."

"All we did was ask a few questions," Leary said. "We didn't take him into custody."

"It's my fault," Jessie spoke up. "I'm the one who wanted to continue investigating Shaw. Emily and Mark were only trying to help. If you're going to discipline anyone here, it should be me."

"That's not true," Leary said, leaning forward. He started to stand up.

"Sit down, Mark." Jessie felt a flash of anger. She didn't need Leary to sacrifice his career for her. "This is on me."

"Maybe we'll discipline all three of you," Warren said.

"That's one way to go," Jessie said. "That might appease Shaw. Or it might not."

"But you have a better idea, of course," Warren said dryly.

"Tie him to Kelly Lee's death. Then he and his company go down, and the DA's Office and PPD are heroes."

No one looked impressed by her plan. "The AID investigation found no evidence suggesting that her death was anything but an accident," Captain Henderson said.

"The AID investigation missed something," Jessie said.

Henderson's gaze swung to Graham. Graham said, "I think it's possible that Jessie is right, Captain."

Henderson made a noise in his throat. He looked at Warren. "I don't like this."

"Neither do I," Warren said.

"If I can bring you evidence proving that Kelly Lee was murdered," Jessie said, "then no one in this room needs to be reprimanded, right?"

Warren and Henderson exchanged another glance. Warren said, "I can give you a few days. But you better believe this is serious, Jessie. If you don't come through, we may have to sacrifice all three of your jobs for the good of the PPD and DA's Office."

Jessie nodded. "I understand."

"Good," Warren said. "Get out. All of you."

They filed out of Warren's office. In the hallway, Graham said, "What the hell was that, Jessie?"

"Did I have a choice?" She looked at her friend. "You realize they were about to suspend, or maybe even fire you, right? Promising them evidence was the only way to save us, after you and Leary went and poked the hornet nest by questioning Shaw."

"There's just one problem," Leary said. "There is no evidence."

"Actually, I think there might be."

Leary and Graham stared at her. "What are you talking about?" Leary said.

But Graham had already caught on. "Vicki Briscoe."

"Exactly," Jessie said.

"Briscoe? As in Ray Briscoe?" Leary said.

"Vicki is his daughter," Jessie said. "She's a doctor—or used to be. Kelly brought a medical malpractice claim against her and she wound up losing her job and her medical license. She wanted revenge. She was following Kelly, *stalking her*, just before her death."

"Doesn't that make her a suspect?" Leary said.

"I don't think she killed Kelly. She wanted to, but I think she would have done it in a more ... hands-on way. She told me—"

"You spoke with her?" Leary looked horrified. "Jessie, these are extremely dangerous people."

"The point is, Vicki Briscoe was *stalking* her. She saw everything Kelly did, everywhere Kelly went, and everyone Kelly talked to, in the days leading to her death. If anyone can lead us to evidence, it's her."

"Why would she help us?" Graham said. "The last time she saw you, she assaulted you."

Leary's eyes bugged out. "She what?"

"We can talk about that later," Jessie said to Leary. To Graham, she said, "Lorena Torres said the Dark Hounds have their headquarters on a former Amish farm. I'm going to drive out to Lancaster and see if I can find Vicki there. Convince her to help us. Or try to, anyway. So are we going to go on pretending we aren't all working on this investigation, or are you two going to come with me?"

23

THEY TOOK Leary's car to make the drive to Lancaster, with Leary driving, Jessie in the passenger seat beside him, and Graham in the back. For most of the ride, they were silent, each of them staring out the windows.

Only an hour outside Philadelphia, and it was like a different world. Pennsylvania Dutch Country was an historic area of Pennsylvania in which thousands of Amish people still maintained their unique, centuries-old way of life. Touristy beds and breakfasts, restaurants selling shoofly pies, and shops offering homemade furniture eventually gave way to windmills, horse stables, and acres and acres of farmland. Even with the windows closed, the odor of horse manure penetrated the car. It was a smell Jessie had always disliked. Soon enough, they approached a horse and buggy riding on the road.

"It's weird," Graham said from the back seat. "They don't use electricity, but their buggies have headlights."

"They also have brakes and a suspension system," Leary said. He carefully maneuvered around the buggy and horse. A man and woman wearing traditional Amish attire—plain and black—sat at the reins. Neither looked over as Leary's car passed them.

"I don't get it," Graham said.

"They don't use public power," Leary said, "but they use batteries. It's not about electricity. Well, not exactly."

"Thanks," Graham said. "That clears it up."

Leary shrugged. "Sorry I don't have a PhD in Amish religious doctrine."

Jessie admired the ability of Leary and Graham to crack jokes en route to the headquarters of a dangerous organized crime family. It must be a cop thing. Her own stomach churned with nausea. She glanced at the GPS app on her phone. *Almost there.*

"Do they have cup holders?" Graham said.

Leary tilted his head up to look at the rearview mirror. "What?"

"In the buggies."

"Good question," Leary said. "When we get back, I'll look that up in my comprehensive treatise on Amish vehicle accessories."

"I think this is the turn," Jessie said.

She was staring at her GPS, but when she looked up, she realized she probably didn't need it. The farm was immediately different from its neighbors. Whereas the Amish farms all appeared neat and well-maintained, the one the motorcycle club used as its base of operations was overgrown and weedy. No cows or horses, or any other animals, in sight. No crops, either. A collection of dark, ominous buildings squatted far back on the land, at the end of a winding gravel road.

She noticed the bantering stopped abruptly. Leary's back seemed to straighten, and she heard the sounds of Graham checking her gun.

Leary's car bumped from pavement onto gravel and their

speed slowed. He pulled up in front of the largest building, shifted the car into park, and turned off the engine. Jessie reached for her door. Her hand trembled. She took a deep breath. Tried to steady herself.

Nothing bad is going to happen. Biker gangs know better than to mess with law enforcement for no reason.

She popped her door open and slid out. The sound of three car doors closing seemed ear-shatteringly loud in the otherwise silent day. She exchanged a look with Leary, then with Graham. They headed for the building together, but stopped short when four men materialized from the shadows at the edges of the structure. They came quickly. The instinct to turn and run almost took over, but Jessie managed to stand her ground. From the corner of her eye, she saw Graham's hand move to her hip and hover there.

"My name is Jessica Black." She spoke quickly, before the encounter could escalate to violence. "I'm with the District Attorney's Office of Philadelphia. We're looking for Vicki Briscoe—"

One of the men gripped her arm. He was bald and had a tattoo of a spiderweb on the pale dome of his head—not exactly Amish style. A second man, short, squat, and wearing a Harley-Davidson baseball cap, approached her with his hands out, then started to pat down her sides. The other two men frisked Leary and Graham, taking their weapons.

"We'll hold onto these, chief," one of them said as he stuck Leary's 9mm into his pocket. "Give it back to you when you leave."

Leary's lips pulled back, showing his teeth, but he didn't object.

Baseball cap was taking his time running his hands along Jessie's torso. "I'm not armed." She jerked away from him.

"You better come with us," Spiderweb said. All four of the

men wore jeans, sleeveless T-shirts, and heavy-looking boots. They marched her, Leary, and Graham into the building.

The light inside the building was low. There was a table, some chairs—wooden furniture that looked finely crafted but misused. Empty beer bottles were scattered on the table's surface. A man sat in one of the chairs. He had a shock of white hair and a matching beard. He stared at the visitors with intense eyes as Spiderweb, Baseball Cap, and the other two bikers marched them into the room.

A wet snoring sound drew Jessie's attention to the corner of the room, where a dog sprawled on the floor. It was a huge Rottweiler, with a thick padding of muscles beneath its black fur. Its eyes were closed and it breathed heavily in its sleep. Even asleep, it brought out a primitive survival response in Jessie. She felt her heart rate jack up and found it difficult to take her eyes off the animal.

"Who are our unexpected visitors?" the white-haired man said.

"This one says she's with the Philly DA," Spiderweb said. "The other two were carrying, Ray."

"That right?" The white-haired man rose fluidly from his chair. Like his underlings, he wore jeans and boots, but where they wore sleeveless T-shirts, he wore a neat button-down shirt with a collar, tucked in. He pulled a pair of glasses from the chest pocket of his shirt and pushed them onto his nose. Peering at her through the lenses, he looked more like a college professor than the ruthless criminal she knew he was.

"You're Ray Briscoe," Jessie said.

"This is a private club. What do you want?"

Leary let out a forced-sounding laugh. "Looks more like a barn than a club."

Ray Briscoe's mouth stretched in a tight line, but he didn't respond to Leary, or even acknowledge him. He kept his gaze on Jessie.

"We were hoping to speak with your daughter," she said.

"Vicki's not here."

Jessie could not discern if he was telling her the truth. She'd known when she decided to make the trip that it might be for nothing, that Vicki Briscoe might be somewhere else. But she had decided to take a chance, mostly because she didn't have any better ideas about where to find the woman. "Can you tell me how to get in touch with her? Do you have her phone number?"

"I have her phone number. I'm not giving it to you. As I said, this is a private club. We're also a private family."

The four men surrounding them closed in, and Jessie braced herself to be forcibly ejected from the premises. "Wait a second," she said. "We're not here as your enemies. We need Vicki Briscoe's help."

Ray Briscoe turned his back on her and walked away. Spiderweb and Baseball Cap began to guide her toward the door. The other men ushered Leary and Graham in the same direction. In the corner, the dog stirred but did not wake.

"We're not ready to leave," Graham said.

Baseball Cap glared at her. "Boss says you are."

Graham rounded on him. "He's not *my* boss."

"We just want to contact Vicki Briscoe," Leary said.

Jessie heard a low moan. Her gaze flew to the Rottweiler, but the dog had not moved. The sound came a second time. A human moan. Coming through the wall.

"Who is that?" Jessie said.

Spideweb jerked her toward the door. "Like the boss said, private club."

The sound came a third time—between a groan and a

whimper. Jessie heard pain. She broke free of the men, hurried past Ray Briscoe and the sleeping dog.

Ray Briscoe reached for her. She felt his fingers brush her shoulder as she passed him. "Where do you think you're going?"

There was a door on the far side of the room. She opened it and found a hallway, narrow and dimly lit. Another groan reached her, closer now. She stepped into the hallway.

"Jessie, wait!" It was Leary's voice, cut short. She glanced back, glimpsed the bikers closing around Leary and Graham, saw Ray Briscoe coming after her. She hurried down the hallway.

"Get back here!" Ray Briscoe's voice. Close behind her.

Jessie stopped in front of another door. The moans were coming from here. She opened it.

Bright light stung her eyes. She blinked, adjusting to the sudden brightness.

What she saw in the glaring clarity of the ceiling lamps made her legs weaken—monitors and stands, a plastic tarp stretched across the floor, and a bloody man on a wheeled hospital bed.

A figure dressed in scrubs and a mask, long red hair tied back and partially covered by a surgical cap, a scalpel gripped in one gloved hand. Blood dripped from the blade. On the bed, the man groaned again. There was a deep incision in his left leg. In a dish beside the bed, metal fragments lay on a blood-soaked paper towel. Jessie felt nausea rush up her throat.

"This is a sterile room!" Vicki Briscoe said through the mask. Her eyes were livid.

From behind Jessie, strong arms pulled her away.

Ray Briscoe threw her into the hallway and kicked the door shut behind them. Jessie looked up into his rage-filled eyes, so similar to his daughter's.

"I told you to leave," he said. "Now you can't."

24

JESSIE'S HEART slammed in her chest. Everything seemed to be moving too quickly. What had she just seen in that room before Ray Briscoe had yanked her out? Blood. Monitors. Scalpel. A makeshift operating room. Vicki Briscoe had been removing something metal—shrapnel or bullet fragments—from a man's leg. She was performing surgery. In a run-down building in the middle of Amish country. Without a medical license.

"Let go of me," Jessie said. She fought to free herself, but Ray Briscoe's grip was unyielding. The narrow hallway—dark after the brightness of the operating room—seemed to close in around her.

"Shut up." His voice came from just behind her right ear. She felt the bristles of his beard touch her neck. His hands tightened on her shoulders and he propelled her roughly forward. She dug in her heels and tried to resist, but he was too strong. She had to walk—her legs unsteady with fear—to avoid falling.

He was forcing her in the wrong direction, away from the building's front door. Where were Leary and Graham?

Ray Briscoe pushed her into a small room at the end of the hall. Inside, Leary and Graham sat in chairs, while the bikers she thought of as Spiderweb and Baseball Cap loomed over them. The other two thugs hovered near the door. Ray Briscoe indicated an empty chair beside Leary and Graham. When Jessie didn't move, he shoved her into the seat.

Fear thrummed through her. "What are we doing in here?" She tried to sound fearless, but there was a waver in her voice that she could not suppress. "I am an assistant district attorney. Think about what you're doing."

"Yeah, you mentioned that." Ray Briscoe turned to the two men at the door. "Any of them move, shoot them." Then he left.

Even though they were far from safe, Jessie felt a rush of relief with Ray Briscoe out of the room. A shuddering breath escaped from her lungs. She looked at Leary and Graham. "Are you guys okay?"

"What's going on?" Leary said. "It sounded like someone was moaning."

Jessie glanced at the four bikers who were watching over them. "Maybe it's better for you if you don't know."

Graham's eyes narrowed. "Whatever you saw—"

The door opened and Ray Briscoe returned. His eyes seemed to simmer with pent-up violence. He breathed, air whistling through his nostrils. "Vicki says she'll talk to you."

"Great," Leary said.

He started to rise. Ray Briscoe lunged forward and thrust him back into his chair. Leary flashed his teeth and looked like he might strike the man, but Spiderweb stepped between them and aimed a nasty-looking revolver at Leary's face. "Careful, boy."

"Not you," Ray Briscoe said. He glared at Jessie. "Miss Assistant DA. She'll talk to you only. Alone."

"No fucking way," Leary said.

Spiderweb smacked the side of his gun against Leary's head.

"No!" Jessie reached toward Leary, but Baseball Cap grabbed

her and held her back. Leary had been knocked halfway out of his chair, almost into Graham's lap. The blow didn't look hard enough to cause major damage, but it did break the skin. A trickle of blood ran down the side of his face. He righted himself and his gaze found Jessie's.

"We should stay together," Leary said through gritted teeth.

"Oh, you can," Ray Briscoe said. "I won't break up the band. But if you insist on staying together, you'll be leaving together without seeing my daughter."

Jessie ignored the man and kept her focus on Leary. "It's okay, Mark. I can do this."

"Jessie, think about this," Graham said. "The last time—"

"I'll be fine," she snapped.

She didn't want to think about the last time she'd encountered Vicki Briscoe. Her arm ached at the memory, and she felt a cold feeling in her stomach. She had hoped to come here as a peaceful visitor seeking advice and assistance, but Ray Briscoe and his thugs had turned the scenario upside down, making her an intruder and a witness to criminal activity. How would Vicki Briscoe react to that? Only one way to find out.

She turned to Ray Briscoe. "Take me to see her."

Ray Briscoe gestured for her to get up, then they exited the room and entered the dark hallway again. He led her to another door and opened it, revealing what looked like a storeroom, with boxes piled against the walls and a card table with two folding chairs in the middle of the room. A bare bulb hung from the ceiling. Ray Briscoe yanked its chain with a hard jerk, and a wan light washed over the table.

"Vicki's very quick in the OR. Sit." Jessie watched the man's face soften. For a second, his expression reminded her of her own father on the day she graduated from law school. Then the moment passed and the hardness in his gaze returned. There was a knock on the door. "Here she is."

Vicki Briscoe still wore blood-streaked scrubs, but she had removed her gloves, mask, and cap, and her red hair was in disarray. Her gaze fell on Jessie as she entered the room. "Give us some privacy, Dad."

He gave his daughter a meaningful look. "She's an assistant DA."

"I know that."

"Don't do anything I wouldn't do."

"I won't."

The father and daughter stared at each other for a second. Then Ray Briscoe nodded and left the room. As soon as he was gone, Vicki Briscoe locked the door after him and turned her attention to Jessie. Jessie rose from her chair, not wanting to be sitting while Vicki loomed over her. That would be too much like their encounter in her apartment.

"Vicki—"

"I thought I warned you to stay away from me."

"You did."

"But here you are. In my home."

Jessie almost pointed out the irony, but thought better of it. Besides, she'd just learned an interesting piece of information. "You live here? With your father and his gang?"

Briscoe looked away, almost with shame. "It's temporary. Tough to pay rent when you don't have a job."

"It looked like you were working a few minutes ago."

Vicki's eyes flashed. "You didn't see anything."

"Alright," Jessie said evenly. "I didn't see anything."

"Why are you here?"

"It's about Kelly Lee."

"You still think I had something to do with her car accident?"

"No. You said you didn't and I'm taking your word for that."

"And yet you brought cops." Briscoe arched an eyebrow.

"Those are my friends. They're here to make sure I don't get hurt."

"That makes me feel warm and fuzzy inside."

"I think I know who the person is who's really behind Kelly's death, but I can't prove it. He's smart. He was careful. He covered his tracks."

Briscoe shrugged. "Oh well."

"But there's one thing he didn't know about, couldn't have prepared for."

Vicki's expression was quizzical. "And what's that?"

"You."

"Me?"

"You told me you were stalking Kelly during the days leading up to her death. Her killer didn't know that. I'm hoping you saw something that might help us prove he killed her."

"Like what?"

"I don't know yet. But if we reconstruct the events leading up to her death, maybe—"

"Why would I help you? That woman ruined my life."

Jessie had anticipated this challenge, had rehearsed her response in her mind during the drive out here—but even so, she hesitated now.

"Why?" Briscoe repeated. She crossed her arms over her chest.

"You were right about Kelly," Jessie said. "At least partly. A lot of her lawsuits were ... questionable."

"Shady," Briscoe said.

"Yes. It looks like she manipulated the legal system, profited by finding the point at which it made more financial sense for a defendant to settle than to fight, even when the defendant had done nothing wrong."

"Like me."

Jessie had no way of knowing whether the medical malpractice claim that had cost Vicki Briscoe her career had been justified or bogus. "If you help me, I'll help you. I'll do whatever I can to convince the medical board to reverse its decision and reinstate your medical license."

"I already talked to lawyers, explored my options. There was nothing they could do. Why would you be any different?"

Jessie felt her back straighten. "For one thing, I'm a respected member of the DA's Office. For another, I'm a damn good lawyer."

Briscoe scoffed, but Jessie saw a familiar look in her eyes. *Hope*.

"Vicki," Jessie said, "what do you have to lose?"

25

WARREN WILLIAMS WAS WORKING in his office when Judge Cynthia Dax swept into the room, looking around at the piles of documents with her nose wrinkled in distaste.

He let out a sigh. First the anger of the police department. Then the complaints from Douglas Shaw. Now a decorated judge. He wondered just how bad this political disaster was going to get. *Real bad*, unless Jessie came through with evidence to back up their meddling in the accident investigation.

Judge Dax was more striking in appearance than Warren had expected—far from the typical dowdy judges he'd become used to. Dax was slim, athletic looking, with long blonde hair—streaked with gray, but still youthful looking—and pretty features. She entered his office as if she owned the place and his usual messy working conditions were an affront to her. She lifted a stack of papers off one of his visitor chairs and transferred it to a clear spot on the floor. Then she sat down and crossed her legs primly.

"I don't know how you can function in an environment like this."

He rocked backward, eliciting a squeal from his chair. "It works for me."

"Does it?" the judge said dubiously.

Warren suddenly wished he'd had a solid night's sleep. His brain felt fuzzy, and he needed every brain cell functioning at peak performance. "Is there something I can help you with, Your Honor?"

"Your office has been overstepping its bounds of late. Specifically, one of your prosecutors, Jessica Black. She harassed me at my courthouse, and has been making slanderous accusations against one of the parties in a trial over which I am presiding. I want her stopped immediately."

"It sounds to me like you're the one making accusations. Slander is a pretty serious word to throw around about one of the Commonwealth's strongest prosecutors."

Dax's expression shifted. Apparently, she had not expected any resistance from him. Warren let himself smile on the inside. He knew he had a reputation as a political toady. While it often irked his pride, it was sometimes valuable to be underestimated —especially by a player like Judge Dax.

She recovered her composure quickly. "If Jessica Black is one of your strongest prosecutors, maybe the DA's Office needs a better homicide chief."

"So now I'm the one you're complaining about?"

Warren had dealt with people like Cynthia Dax before—complainers who were never satisfied and who viewed everyone who was not their advocate as their enemy. He would have liked nothing more than to throw her out of here. But it wasn't as easy as lifting his phone and having her removed from his sight. Dax was a judge, and a politically connected one at that. Warren's job was largely political. Every action he took needed to be weighed for its political consequences—consequences to him, to the

District Attorney of Philadelphia, Jesus Rivera, and to the DA's Office. He folded his hands in front of him.

"Why don't you tell me what Jessie Black said that upset you?"

"I'm not upset, Warren. I am offended and annoyed. Your prosecutor has attempted to insert herself in the Rowland case. That's not acceptable."

"That sounds kind of tenuous." Warren felt a wave of relief that he hoped didn't show on his face. At least Jessie hadn't made any overt move against the judge.

"When I'm done, the only thing that will be tenuous is your future."

"What are you suggesting that I do to help you, Judge Dax?"

"For now, make Black stand down. I don't ever want to see that woman again, or hear her voice. Get her off my back."

"No problem. I understand Noah Snyder is representing the Rowlands now. Jessie is no longer involved in the case."

Dax eyed him with open skepticism, but said nothing.

"You said, 'for now,'" Warren said. "Is there more?"

"No. But if Black's interference continues, then I will have no choice but to escalate this to my friends in the mayor's office. Make no mistake, Warren. I can cause serious problems for you and your office. And I will."

"I thought we already covered the part of the conversation where you throw around empty threats."

Dax raised her chin. "I trust you'll do the right thing."

Warren watched her rise from the chair. She stood over him for a moment, again looking with distaste at the documents spread everywhere on his desk. Then she turned away and made her way out of the room. Warren waited until she was gone before letting out a pent-up breath. Then he thought about his next move.

26

VICKI BRISCOE ESCORTED Jessie back to the room where Leary and Graham were being held. She found them still sitting in their chairs, with Ray Briscoe's goons hovering at their shoulders.

Jessie turned to Briscoe. "Can you give us a minute alone, please?"

Briscoe turned to leave, motioning for the bikers to follow her. "Don't keep me waiting."

When the door closed, Leary and Graham shot up from their seats. "Are you okay?" Leary said.

"Everything's fine."

"She agreed to help?" Graham said, her voice laced with disbelief.

"We worked out an arrangement."

"What does that mean?" Leary said.

"You two need to leave," Jessie said.

Leary stared at her. "What about you?"

"I'm going with Vicki."

"Like hell you are. Do you not see how much danger you've already put yourself in today? You're a lawyer, not a cop. You're not equipped to deal with a person like Vicki Briscoe alone. Emily, back me up here."

Graham crossed her arms over her chest. "I trust Jessie to make her own decisions."

"Are you serious?" Leary's voice rose. "Is this because you're still pissed off at her for trying to help Kelly Lee?"

Graham seemed to bristle at the accusation. "No, actually, it's because I have faith in her."

"You're saying I don't?"

"I'm saying you have a hero complex. An I'm-a-big-strong-man-protecting-my-woman thing. It's a little over-the-top, Mark."

Leary's face twisted. "It's not a complex. It's common sense!"

"We're not going to debate this," Jessie said, cutting off their argument. "I know what I'm doing. Mark, we've been through a lot together. You know I'm not a damsel in distress."

"I never said you were."

"I'm going back to Philly with Vicki. She's going to take me on a tour of Kelly's final days. Hopefully, I'll find something useful. If I don't, we have bigger problems."

"Why can't we come with you?" Leary said.

"Because Vicki doesn't want you to."

"That's not a red flag for you?"

"It is, and I'll be careful."

Graham took Leary by the arm. "Mark, let's go."

Leary didn't look happy about it, but he went. Jessie followed him and Graham outside.

It was still daytime, but night was coming and the unkempt farmland looked gloomy. Spiderweb returned their weapons, and Leary and Graham climbed into Leary's car. Jessie felt Leary's anxious gaze on her. She hoped she wasn't making a huge mistake by not listening to him.

She watched the car drive toward the main road and listened

to the sound of tires crunching gravel. When the car was out of sight, she turned to Briscoe with what she hoped was a confident expression. "You ready to go?"

Briscoe pointed to a nearby structure. "My car is in the garage over there." It turned out to be a sleek, black Mercedes. Jessie walked to the passenger side and opened the door as Briscoe took the wheel. The vehicle was as spotlessly clean on the inside as it was on the outside. Briscoe drummed her fingers against the steering wheel.

"Nice car," Jessie said.

"I was a surgeon at a major Philadelphia hospital when I started the lease." Briscoe's tone sounded defensive.

"I didn't mean—"

"Didn't mean *nice car for an unemployed, unlicensed doctor living with her dad?*"

Briscoe's fingers stopped drumming. She stared at Jessie with an intensity that made Jessie wish Leary and Graham were still with her.

"No. I didn't mean that."

Briscoe continued to stare. Then her fingers resumed their drumming. She turned away from Jessie and looked out the windshield. "Let's get going. It's a long ride back to Philly."

Traffic was light, and the ride didn't actually take that long. When the Philadelphia skyline came into view, Jessie felt some of the tension in her body ease. A sense of safety—probably a false sense, she knew—made her feel less at the mercy of this woman. They entered the city and she saw other cars, pedestrians, signs of normal life.

Jessie asked Briscoe to retrace the locations she'd seen while stalking Kelly. Their first stop was a small office complex down the street from Thomas Jefferson University Hospital in Center City. Briscoe paused in front of the entrance where a plain, white sign was affixed to the brick wall. Reading it, Jessie felt a jolt of adrenaline. "It's a doctor's office."

Briscoe looked at her with a curious expression. "That's exciting to you?"

"Before she died, Kelly told me she consulted a doctor about the Rowland case. At that point in time, she thought it was a medical malpractice claim, and she wanted this doctor's opinion about whether the Rowlands' pediatrician had misdiagnosed their son."

Briscoe's lip curled. "So he's one of those doctors who gets paid to testify against other doctors."

"They're called expert witnesses. I guess there was probably one at your trial."

Briscoe shrugged. "The hospital's insurance company settled, so I never had to listen to the expert in my trial testify in court. I read her report, though." Briscoe quickly looked away, but not before Jessie glimpsed the pain in her eyes.

"Kelly never told me her expert witness's name. She just referred to him as a doctor. I'm pretty sure she said, 'he.'"

"The court won't tell you the guy's name?"

She thought of Judge Dax. "The judge hasn't been very helpful. But even if she wanted to tell me, she probably doesn't know. The discovery phase of the trial hasn't started yet, so Kelly wasn't required to disclose that information to the court." Kelly Lee's crash had occurred before the identification of expert witnesses, which would be part of the discovery schedule once Judge Dax set a trial date. Jessie had asked Kelly's assistant, Cheyenne, but the woman had not known. Without access to Kelly's own files, and with no expert witness identifications in the pleadings, Jessie and Snyder had no way to know the name of the expert witness who'd found the excessive levels of formaldehyde in the toy. "If Kelly was visiting this doctor days before her death, maybe he was her expert witness. That would be a big help."

"Stephen Adkins, M.D.," Briscoe said, reading the sign.

A sports car honked and swerved around them. Jessie realized they'd been idling at the curb for a minute, maybe longer. "I'm getting out. Do you want to circle the block? I'm not sure how long I'll be."

"I can find a spot and we can both go in," Briscoe said.

"I think it's better if I do this part alone."

Briscoe's eyes narrowed. "Sitting in the car waiting for you doesn't sound like a fun time to me."

Fun? Jessie felt a stirring of uneasiness. "I never said this would be fun. I said if you help me, I'll help you."

"Don't keep me waiting."

Jessie got out of the Mercedes and hurried inside the building.

27

EMILY GRAHAM WATCHED LEARY DRIVE. Since starting the engine, he'd been silent, staring straight ahead. She could practically feel the emotional turmoil radiating off of him.

They drove through a rustic town with Amish shops—furniture, food, a bed-and-breakfast. "Do you think we should stop for shoofly pie?" she asked. When he didn't respond, she added, "You're the Amish expert, remember?"

The muscles of his face seemed to bunch up.

"You're giving me the silent treatment?" she said. "Mark, I know you're worried about her. I'm worried about her, too."

He continued to stare straight ahead. "If anything happens to her." He left the sentence unfinished.

"Jessie is a grown woman, a professional. She deals with criminals every day."

"Not like this."

Silence filled the car. Amish countryside eventually gave way to more twenty-first-century civilization.

"What are you going to do?" Graham said.

"Head back to the DA's Office, try to distract myself with

work so I don't think about the love of my life driving around with a psychopath. Where should I drop you?"

Graham didn't want to admit it, but she had the same idea—bury herself in work and try not to think about Jessie being in danger. "The Roundhouse."

"You sure? It's getting late."

She tilted her head so she could glance through the windshield at the darkening sky. It didn't change her mind. "Yes."

"You got it." He drove to police headquarters and stopped the car at the curb. Graham reached for the door handle, then paused and looked back at Leary. "Jessie will be okay."

Leary nodded.

Graham climbed out of his car and headed for the entrance to the Roundhouse. The sky was getting darker by the minute, and she knew the homicide squad room would be quiet. She had some reports to work on—a task she despised, but one she hoped would divert her attention away from Jessie and ease the fluttering in her stomach.

As she approached the building, a man stepped out of the shadows. Graham stopped short. It was Ross Reid, the AID detective.

"Buy you a drink?" he said.

She tried not to look startled. "How did you know I'd be here?"

"I didn't. I was at the Roundhouse and saw you as I was walking out."

"But now you want to buy me a drink."

He let out an impatient sound. "If you have somewhere you need to be—"

"Actually, I could use a drink," she said.

Five minutes later they were sitting side-by-side at a bar. He ordered a tequila and soda and asked what she wanted.

"Yuengling," she said, indicating the tap. She wanted to stay sober tonight, in case Jessie needed her, but she didn't think one beer would hurt. In her current frame of mind, it could only help.

The bartender, a middle-aged man with a salt-and-pepper beard, gave them their drinks. "You want to settle up now or run a tab?"

"Tab," Reid said.

"You got it."

Reid seemed to wait until the bartender moved on, then brought his glass to his mouth. Ice cubes rattled as he took a long drink.

"What's going on?" Graham said. She took a sip from her pint glass. "You look like there's something you want to say."

He laughed. "You could tell? I see why you're good at your job."

"Well?"

"There is something I'd like to get off my chest."

"You're going to tell me again what an arrogant homicide detective I am?"

"No." Reid smiled at her, but his expression seemed morose. "And I'm sorry about saying that. You seem like a decent person. A decent cop."

"Gee, thanks."

"I'm serious. I'm trying to apologize here."

Graham offered a smile of her own. "Okay. I know. It's been a tough day. Apology accepted."

He took another long drink of his tequila and soda, and she sensed he was building up the courage to continue. She drank her beer, giving him time.

"There's something I didn't tell you before, when we spoke at the gym," he said.

"About Lee's crash?"

Reid nodded. "I've been ... well ... not exactly hiding something. Nothing like that. But...."

Graham put down her glass. "Why don't you start at the beginning."

"The beginning?"

"You said there was nothing suspicious about Lee's accident. Was that the truth?"

"Yes." He said it without hesitation, but then he added, "Mostly."

"Mostly?"

"It was an unusually bad accident, but not a suspicious one. When a car hits a brick wall at high speed, well...." He waved his glass, which was now empty except for ice cubes. "The results aren't going to be pretty, you know?"

"Lee's car exploded. That's normal?"

"Her car didn't explode. It burned. There's a difference. You can have a very intense fire in a car wreck. The engine is hot, you've got fuel, other fluids. Lots of flammable plastic and foam. All it takes is a sheared fuel line, a puncture in the gas tank, and a spark...." His voice trailed off.

"You said you didn't find any evidence of explosives or explosive devices."

"That's right."

"And no evidence of tampering with the car."

"Correct."

She rocked on her stool. "I'm a little confused here, Ross. What didn't you tell me?"

He put down his drink. Took a deep breath. "I found a brick in the well under the driver's seat. It's probably nothing. Lee's car collided with a brick wall and did a lot of damage. Her front windshield was destroyed and a brick could have easily tumbled into the car after the impact. But...."

"But?" She prompted.

"I looked at the wall during the incident, and at photos of it afterward. There's no missing brick. Also, the color of the wall and the color of the brick I found in the car don't match."

"Could someone have used the brick to weight down the gas pedal and cause the accident? Force Lee's car to race headfirst into the building?"

"Obviously, I've been thinking about that. Especially after you visited me at the gym. But it doesn't fit, right? I mean, it's not like Kelly Lee's arms and legs were tied up. If someone put a brick on the pedal, she could have just kicked it off."

"What if she was unconscious? Drugged?"

"It's possible." Reid shrugged. "The medical examiner wasn't able to determine much. Because of the impact and the fire, there wasn't much left of the body to examine."

"You logged the brick?"

"Of course. But in the end, it didn't change my conclusion."

Graham finished her beer slowly, thinking. "Thank you for telling me this, Ross."

"Does it help? You know, with whatever you're doing?"

"I'm not sure yet, but it might." She slid off the stool. "Thanks for the beer."

"Wait. You don't want to stay for another round?"

"I can't tonight." She looked at him, seeing him differently now. "But maybe another time?"

He smiled. "I'd like that."

28

Mark Leary sat at his desk in the DA's Office. He lowered his head and rubbed his temples. The hour was still early, but he was dead tired. Emotionally spent. He took a breath and forced his attention to the Philadelphia Inquirer article on his screen.

It was one of dozens of web pages to which a Google search for *Ray Briscoe* had led him. His original searches, for *Vicki Briscoe* and *Victoria Briscoe*, had not returned any relevant hits, and so far, the daughter's name had not appeared in any of the articles about her father. Leary supposed this should comfort him, but it did not.

He had not really spoken to the woman, or even seen her for more than a few minutes. Still, he sensed there was something ... off-balance about her. And even if his instincts were wrong— and they rarely were—Briscoe lived with her crime figure father on property run by a criminal syndicate. She'd admitted to Jessie that she had been stalking Kelly Lee with a desire to hurt her. These were not exactly facts describing a normal human being.

She was dangerous, and Jessie was alone with her.

So what was he going to do about it?

He rubbed his forehead again. What could he do? Possibly

he could trace her location by using her mobile phone signal, but she was already chafing at his protectiveness. If he tried to track her location and she found out, that might be the end of their relationship.

So what? Isn't her life more important than the relationship?

Maybe. But if there was another way to help her, to keep her safe, and not lose her at the same time, that would obviously be preferable. He loved her.

The sound of his cell phone vibrating roused him from his thoughts. He turned and saw Warren Williams's name appear on the screen. Great. Just what he needed.

"Listen, Warren. Fire me if you need to. I understand how these things work. But don't sacrifice Jessie. She's too valuable for this office—you know I'm right—and she also deserves better from you. She—"

Warren cleared his throat loudly. "Thanks for your unbiased opinion, but if you don't mind, I actually have some work for you to do. You know, as an employee of the DA's Office?"

Leary glanced at his watch. "Now?"

"You really want to help Jessie?"

Leary straightened in his chair. "You know I do."

"Then help *me*. I need your detective skills."

"I'm listening."

"There's a judge of the court of common pleas, by the name of Cynthia Dax. She's the judge assigned to the Rowland case that Kelly Lee was working on before her accident."

"Okay."

"Jessie visited her. Apparently, she didn't make a good impression. Dax came here and threatened me. She wants action taken against Jessie."

"Seriously? Can anything else go wrong?"

"Something else can always go wrong, but let's focus on one problem at a time. I need to get Dax off my back."

"You mean you're not going to penalize Jessie?" Leary felt some of the tension in his shoulders loosen. He leaned back.

"I didn't say that. But if I decide to, it will be my decision. It won't be because some judge pushed me around. I need something on Dax. Dirt. A skeleton in her closet. Most people have something to hide, even judges. Find me something I can use to force Dax to back off. And find it quickly."

Leary was already rising from his chair. "I'll start right now," he said, and ended the call.

29

It was early evening when Jessie opened the door and stepped inside the medical office of Stephen Adkins, M.D. She was relieved the office was still open. The waiting room was quiet, the line of uncomfortable-looking chairs vacant. A woman sat behind the reception desk, squinting at a computer monitor and typing. Without looking away from her screen, she said, "We're about to close up."

"My name is Jessica Black. I'm an assistant district attorney."

That got the woman's attention. "What's this about?"

"I'm looking into a matter involving a lawyer named Kelly Lee. She was here a few days ago. I'd like to speak with whomever Kelly Lee met with when she was here."

"Can't give you that information. HIPAA."

Jessie wasn't overly familiar with the privacy law, but didn't think it applied here. "I'm not asking you for patient information. I just want to know who Kelly spoke with when she came here."

The woman sighed, removed her hands from her keyboard, and peered at Jessie as if she were a moron. "That *is* patient information."

"Kelly was a patient here?"

The woman looked suddenly angry, as if she had just been tricked into giving away highly confidential information. Jessie supposed that was an improvement over the are-you-a-moron look.

"I think you should leave," the woman said.

"Listen to me. Kelly Lee died a few days ago in a car accident. I'm trying to help the lawyer who's replacing her on a big trial, to put the pieces together so that he can successfully continue the trial without her. I think she might have consulted with the doctor here as an expert for that case. Dr. Adkins? That's why I want to know whom she spoke with."

The woman shook her head. "If that's what you're looking for, I can tell you that you're in the wrong place. Kelly was here for her annual physical, if you must know. She wasn't here to talk about a case. Now, that's probably more than I'm even allowed to tell you and I'm certainly not going to tell you anything else."

Jessie nodded, hoping her disappointment didn't show on her face. She should have known that Kelly's visit to this doctor's office might not have any relevance to the trial against Boffo, or to her supposed accident, but she'd been so desperate for any step forward, she'd convinced herself she would find useful information here.

"Thank you," she said. "I appreciate you telling me that. I guess I did come to the wrong place."

Back at the car, Briscoe looked at Jessie expectantly as Jessie slid into the passenger seat and closed the door. "Dead end."

"Bummer," Briscoe said without the slightest hint of sympathy.

Jessie checked her watch. Time was slipping away. "What's our next stop?"

Briscoe shifted the Mercedes into drive and pulled into traffic. "After Kelly Lee was in the doctor's office for an hour or so, she came out and I followed her to University City."

"Where in University City?"

"A bookstore. One of those bookstore coffee house places, but not Barnes & Noble. This was like a mom-and-pop version on Sansom Street."

Jessie had spent a lot of time in coffee shops in University City during her three years of law school at the University of Pennsylvania, but since beginning her job at the DA's Office, she had not had many occasions to return to that neighborhood. She was sure that most of the coffee shops had changed in the ten-plus years since she'd frequented the area. "A bookstore and coffee shop in University City," Jessie said, thinking aloud. "That's pretty far from her office. What was she doing there?"

"Meeting with someone. A gray-haired woman in a suit."

"Can you be more specific? Did you notice any other details about the woman?"

"No."

Jessie watched through the car window as Briscoe navigated west. The ride took fifteen minutes in traffic. Briscoe found parking on the street, and they entered the bookstore together. The smell of fresh coffee was a welcome sensation, and Jessie spontaneously headed toward the coffee bar near the back of the store. Briscoe followed.

"Do you want anything?" Jessie said.

"Kind of late for coffee, isn't it?"

"Not for me."

Briscoe shrugged. "Cappuccino, if you're buying."

They ordered their drinks from a guy who looked like a kid to Jessie. Maybe a college student at one of the several schools that gave University City its name. After charging Jessie's credit card, he handed the drinks to Jessie, who passed the cappuccino to Briscoe.

"*Ah!*" Briscoe shoved her cup onto the counter, almost dropping it. She lifted her palm and winced.

"I guess they're a little hot," Jessie said.

"These are surgeon's hands, you idiot. At least, they used to be, and I'm hoping they will be again." Briscoe stared at her palm, her face a mask of worry. After a few seconds, Briscoe seemed to calm down. She picked up her cup. "I'm alright."

"Good."

They stepped away from the counter. Steam rose from Jessie's cup. She took a tentative sip. The coffee was very hot and had a slightly burnt taste, but was still pretty good.

Briscoe said, "You're going to think I'm bullshitting you, but see that lady over there?" A brown-haired, mousy woman browsed the books in the romance aisle. "That's the woman I saw Kelly Lee meet." She took a swig of her cappuccino.

"In the car, you said she had gray hair."

"That's her."

"You're sure?"

Briscoe shot her a frustrated glare over the rim of her cup.

"Okay," Jessie said. "I'm going to talk to her. Stay here." Briscoe's eyes flashed an objection, but Jessie headed over to the aisle of romance books before she could argue. A second later, she realized Briscoe was walking beside her anyway. They reached the woman at the same time, and Jessie said, "Excuse me. This is going to sound strange, but my name is Jessica Black. I think a friend of mine met you here the other day. Kelly Lee."

The woman's face lit up. "Do you know Kelly from Penn Law?"

"Yes," Jessie said. "Is that how you know her?"

The woman seemed delighted. "I was her Torts professor."

"They have cooking classes in law school?" Briscoe said.

The professor stared at her. "I guess you're not a lawyer. A tort is a kind of legal claim. An act or omission that harms another."

Briscoe's eyes seemed to darken. "I was joking." She pulled a book from the shelf and flipped through its pages as if it were much more interesting than the conversation.

"My name is Hazel Little," the professor said, turning to face Jessie again. They shook hands.

"Did Kelly meet with you to talk about law?" Jessie said.

"She had some questions about the standard for certifying a class under Pennsylvania law. We spoke for half an hour, maybe forty-five minutes. I emailed her some articles, too. She's always been very bright."

"Did Kelly tell you anything specific about the case she was working on?"

"Not really. I think she mentioned it involved toys? We didn't talk about specifics. She was interested in the current case law on the subject."

"If I give you my email address, do you think you could email those articles to me?"

"I don't see why not. Would that be helpful to you as well?"

"Extremely helpful. Thank you."

They said goodbye and left. Outside, Briscoe said, "I thought you were trying to find Kelly's murderer, not bone up on your legal knowledge."

"I've got a few different things going on. It's complicated." Jessie didn't feel like explaining to Briscoe the situation with Noah Snyder, and the legal work she'd become responsible for handling.

"You must be really fun at parties."

"Where did Kelly go after she met with the professor at the bookstore?"

They walked toward Briscoe's car. Briscoe unlocked it and they both got inside. "What about my thing?"

"What are you talking about?" Jessie said.

"You said you have a few different things going on. What about my thing—getting my medical license reinstated?"

"I'll work on that after you help me. That was the deal."

"After I help you, I won't have any leverage."

"I'm good to my word."

"Your word?" Briscoe dismissed the idea with a shake of her head, as if it were hopelessly quaint. "What's that worth?"

Jessie thought it was worth everything, but she didn't bother trying to argue the point with Vicki Briscoe. "How about if I have a DA's Office detective look into the claim against you? Dig around for some holes?"

Briscoe nodded carefully. "That would be a good start. More than the hospital's insurance company bothered to do, I'm sure."

"What did the plaintiff allege you did wrong?"

"I didn't do anything wrong. I performed his surgical procedure flawlessly. But this procedure always has possible complications. I warned the patient about the risks and he wanted the procedure anyway. Later, he and Lee lied that I never told him about the complications, that I failed to get his informed consent. Apparently, it's a common lawyer trick." Briscoe's face twisted in a look of disgust, which Jessie tried to ignore.

"Give me all the details."

30

VICKI BRISCOE DROPPED Jessie off at her apartment building. The Mercedes drove away, but Jessie stood outside in the chilly darkness, unable, for the moment, to enter the building. There was a sinking feeling in her stomach.

For all her running around over the past few days, she seemed to be moving backward rather than forward. All she'd wanted to do was ensure that Kelly Lee's accident received scrutiny, but now she was responsible for so much more—doing the legal work on the Rowlands' case, finding a basis to convince the state medical board to reinstate Vicki Briscoe's license, and personally investigating Kelly's death. She was no closer to accomplishing anything, and she'd managed to anger Warren Williams and Captain Henderson, and put her own career, as well as Leary's and Graham's, at risk.

For the first time since she'd stared in horror at the steaming husk of Kelly Lee's crushed automobile, Jessie felt an awful gnawing in the pit of her stomach. Had she made a huge mistake?

No.

She couldn't allow herself to succumb to fear and doubt. The facts had not changed. She still believed that Kelly Lee was killed—that her supposed accident had actually been orchestrated by a killer and then covered up by the police, either intentionally or through a negligent investigation by an AID team biased against the victim. Only one thing had changed, and that was that proving Kelly had been murdered was turning out to be harder than she'd anticipated. So what? Jessie had never fled from a challenge before, and she wasn't going to start now. She wasn't afraid of hard work. She embraced it. Throughout her life, her willingness to do the hard work was exactly what had given her an edge and enabled her to succeed.

She would take these challenges one at a time, knock down each hurdle between her and justice. Tomorrow morning, hopefully she would receive an email from Kelly's professor with the documents she'd sent Kelly to help with the Rowland case. Jessie would begin there.

She entered the building and walked to her first-floor apartment. She took a breath, unlocked the door, and entered. She wasn't surprised to find Leary on the couch, waiting up for her. She was too tired right now to deal with the look of concern on his face.

"Hey," he said.

She dropped her keys on the counter in the kitchenette. She considered joining him on the couch, but wasn't ready to be peppered with questions about her night. "I'm going to sleep," she said.

"It's only 10."

"I'm exhausted."

"Everything went okay tonight? With Briscoe?"

She could hear in his cautious tone his attempt to approach the subject tactfully, and that only made her more reluctant to talk. A weary sigh escaped before she could suppress it. She saw him wince.

Just be honest with him. She walked to the couch and sat down. He took her hand. His touch felt wonderful, as always, warm and strong. *Just tell him you need him to give you some space.* She tried to think of the best way to phrase that.

Leary spoke before she could. He said, "I'm sorry. I know I've been acting overprotective of you. It must feel like ... I don't know. Like I'm treating you like you can't take care of yourself. And we both know you can."

He squeezed her hand. She squeezed him back. "Leary...."

"I just can't bear the thought of losing you," he said. "Or maybe Emily's right and I just want to be a hero."

"Sometimes I like you to be the hero."

"Yeah, too bad I obviously can't tell when that is."

"I guess I'm not that great at communicating that."

"You are mysterious."

She kissed him. She felt his body straighten with surprise. Then he put a hand on her head, threading his fingers through her hair, and kissed her back.

"Maybe if we had a secret phrase," he said, his lips brushing hers.

"Like *tomato*?"

"Sure, why not? Nothing screams *Help me!* like a fresh, ripe tomato."

She laughed. "Well, I don't need any tomatoes right now, okay? But I'll let you know if I do." They kissed again.

Leary smiled. "Seems like a long time since we kissed like that."

"Too long."

He leaned back against the couch cushions. "I need to tell you something. I got a call from Warren today. Judge Dax complained to him about your involvement in the Rowland case. She threatened to make trouble for the DA's Office."

Jessie cringed.

"You're surprised?"

"I know I didn't exactly dazzle her with my charm, but I didn't think she would come after me."

"Well, she did. Warren's not about to roll over, though. He's going to push back, and I'm going to help him."

"How?"

"Leverage. Everyone has weak points, even judges. We'll find hers and use it to force her to back off."

Jessie sighed. She didn't like the idea—what Leary was describing sounded too close to blackmail—but she didn't have any better suggestions. And she believed she was in the right. She'd done nothing except try to ensure that Kelly's death did not compromise the Rowlands' legal case.

"Don't feel bad about it," he said, as if reading her thoughts. "She threatened to use her political clout to harm you, Warren, and the DA's Office. She's bad."

"Sounds that way." She paused, then said, "I need your help with something else."

"Anything."

"Vicki Briscoe only agreed to help me because I promised her I would help her get her medical license reinstated. She said the claim Kelly brought against her was bogus, but that the insurance company settled instead of fighting it. I was hoping you could—"

"Do some detective work?" He grinned. "That's what I do best."

"I think there's something you do even better."

Jessie leaned toward him again, moving in for another kiss. His grin widened.

31

WHEN JESSIE'S alarm went off the next morning, the first thing she did was check her phone for a new email. Sure enough, the one she was hoping for was there, sent a few hours after she fell asleep the night before—an email from Professor Hazel Little, with a Penn Law email address, and several attachments.

Jessie swung her legs over the side of the bed and hurried to the desk in the corner of the bedroom. The attachments were PDFs, and she wanted to open them on a screen large enough to make them readable. She didn't intend to study the documents in depth right now—she could tell from the file names that they were judicial decisions and legal articles, the kind of reading material she could tackle better at her desk at the DA's Office, with a cup of coffee in her hand—but she couldn't resist a quick preview.

A grunt sounded from the bed. Leary rolled over, tucking the covers around him. Jessie tried to minimize the noise as she started her laptop, typed in her password, and brought up the email.

Hi Jessica. Wonderful to meet you. I hope you find these helpful. Best of luck, Hazel Little.

Jessie typed a quick thank-you note and sent it back to the professor. Then she opened the first attachment, a recent decision involving a class certification on appeal. It appeared to include a thorough legal analysis, with plenty of case law cited.

She skimmed at first, then slowed down when she realized the facts of the case were similar to those of the Rowland matter. Her finger touched the scroll wheel of her mouse and she learned forward, reading.

The sound of a throat clearing brought her back to the moment. She looked up from the screen. Leary stood beside her, naked except for a pair of boxer briefs. A toothbrush stuck out of his mouth.

Jessie's gaze went to the clock at the corner of the computer screen. Since she'd gotten out of bed, an hour had passed.

Leary pulled the toothbrush from his mouth. "Good morning."

"Hey," she said. She was suddenly conscious that she was still in her pajamas and had not even brushed her teeth. "I lost track of time. These documents Kelly's old professor sent over … they're going to be a huge help."

"I'll make coffee."

She looked up, smiled at him. "You always know just what to say."

He left the bedroom. A moment later, she heard the sound of the coffeemaker percolating in the kitchenette. The smell of coffee beans reached the bedroom and she took a deep breath, savoring it.

Returning her attention to the computer, she pulled up the second attachment. Like the first, it was a Pennsylvania case, reasonably recent, factually on-point, binding precedent. She almost couldn't believe her good fortune. These documents would make her work for Snyder much easier. By leading Jessie to Professor Hazel Little, Vicki Briscoe had really come through.

What about my side of the bargain?

Leary returned to the bedroom with a mug of coffee in each hand. He held one out to her and she took it gratefully, cradling the hot cup in her hands. She breathed in the steam and then took a long sip.

"Perfect."

"I don't know if I'm *perfect*." He grinned down at her. "But I have my moments."

"Ha ha. I meant the coffee, but you're not bad either."

He drank from his own mug. "So you think you can win this case?"

"It's just a motion at this stage. Two motions, actually. And it's Noah Snyder who needs to win them, not me. But I think I can give him the legal ammunition he needs to do it."

"Good."

"You're going to look into Vicki Briscoe's malpractice case today, right?"

"You mind if I put on some clothes first?" He gestured at his mostly naked body.

"Sorry. I don't mean to be pushy. I just want Vicki Briscoe to continue helping me. She already led me to Professor Hazel Little. But I'm really hoping she'll lead me to Kelly's killer."

Leary's body seemed to become tense. "Let's hope she leads you to the *identity* of the killer. Not sure I want you and the killer actually coming face-to-face. Not that I don't have total confidence in you—"

She smiled around the rim of her coffee mug. "It's okay, Leary. I know what you meant. And I agree. I'm not looking for a showdown either."

"Good."

She rose from her chair. "I should take a shower. I'll finish going through the files at the office."

A buzzing noise drew both their attentions to Jessie's phone, which she'd left on the desk beside her computer. She didn't recognize the phone number of the incoming call, but *Devon, Pennsylvania* appeared on the screen. That was the town in which the Rowlands lived.

Jessie picked up. "Jessica Black."

"This is Ken Rowland." The man's voice, raw and angry, made Jessie freeze. "You have a lot of nerve."

"What's wrong?" Jessie handed her coffee mug to Leary and stepped away from the desk.

"You said you were going to find us a new lawyer who would help us win our case. But this guy Snyder—"

Jessie closed her eyes, experiencing a feeling of dread only Snyder could instill. "Listen, I know he's a little unconventional —crass, even rude sometimes—but underneath all that, Noah Snyder is an excellent lawyer. You have to trust me—"

"An excellent lawyer?" Ken Rowland barked out a laugh. "An excellent lawyer is supposed to have his clients' best interests at heart, right? Not stab them in the back."

The feeling of dread intensified. "Is it possible there was a ... some kind of miscommunication? How do you feel that he stabbed you in the back?"

"Oh, I don't know." Ken's voice dripped sarcasm. "Maybe when he met with Douglas Shaw behind our backs and worked out a nice little deal to make our case go away in exchange for a payoff?"

"He discussed a possible settlement?" Jessie tried to keep her voice neutral. She knew the Rowlands had no interest in settling, and she thought she'd made that clear to Snyder, but it was still common practice. "I'm sure he only met with Shaw as a courtesy. He knows your position."

"He showed up this morning with a ten page document!" Jessie heard the sound of rustling paper on the other end of the line. "Settlement and Release Agreement," Ken Rowlands read.

"It's already signed by Shaw, and there are signature lines for Deanna and me. Snyder said the judge approved it, too. He told us to sign it!"

The dread turned to anger. Jessie felt her jaw tighten. "Did you?"

"Of course not! I threw the bastard out of our house!"

"Okay. Good. The contract isn't valid without your signature."

"No kidding. We want a new lawyer."

"I don't think you should switch lawyers." Jessie glanced at Leary, who was watching her with a concerned expression. She touched his arm, rolled her eyes, and silently mouthed *Snyder*. He nodded with understanding and moved to the bathroom.

"Why not?"

Jessie didn't want to admit that Snyder had been her last option after calling all of the other personal injury lawyers she knew. She also didn't want to admit that she was personally doing the legal work. "Like I said, Noah is unconventional, but he's good. I'll talk to him and straighten this out. Do you trust me?"

Ken Rowland seemed to hesitate. Then he said, "Yes, we trust you."

"Then please give me a chance to fix this."

She ended the call and, still in her pajamas, called Noah Snyder. When he picked up, she heard noise on the line and assumed he'd answered in his car, probably heading away from the Rowlands' house.

"They called you, huh?" Snyder said. "Fucking tattletales."

The rage she'd bottled up finally let loose. "A settlement agreement, Noah? Really? What the hell were you thinking?"

She heard his calm, unconcerned laugh, a sound which only infuriated her more. "I was thinking my clients could obtain an excellent settlement, avoid a trial they'd probably lose—

assuming the case even survives summary judgment and makes it to trial—and move on with their lives."

"They don't want to settle. You know that."

"They're idiots, Jessie. It's my job to protect them from their own stupidity."

"They're not stupid. They're angry and grieving. Can't you understand that?"

"What I understand is that Judge Dax is going to deny the motion to certify a class—which leaves the Rowlands on their own—and then grant Boffo's motion for summary judgment, which will throw what's left of the case into the garbage can. Is that a result that's going to help their anger and grief?"

"It doesn't have to go that way. I'm working on the reply brief —like you asked me to—and I think I have some arguments that can help us prevail on both motions."

"Oh yeah?" Instead of sounding relieved, Snyder sounded incredulous. Was the idea that they could win really so unfathomable to him?

"Yeah." She threw the word back at him. "Unless you know something I don't know—"

"As a matter of fact, I do," he said, cutting her off. "I know that Judge Dax just put a hearing on the calendar for 2 PM this afternoon to hear arguments on both motions."

"She can't do that."

"She *did* do that. So you have what? A few hours to research and draft your reply brief, and prepare me to argue both motions? You're good, but I doubt you're that good."

Jessie felt the air go out of her lungs.

"You there?" Snyder said. His voice softened. "Look, I'm sorry. I know this sucks. The legal world is a dirty place. Let's talk to the Rowlands together. We can convince them that a settlement makes sense."

"No. I'll get the work done this morning," Jessie said. "I can do it."

"Jessie, be reasonable."

"Just show up at court at 2 PM. I'll do the rest."

But how she was going to do that, she had no idea.

LEARY FOUND Noah Snyder in the back room of a cigar lounge in Northeast Philly. At 11:00 AM on a weekday, the lawyer had the space to himself, but he'd managed to fill the air with a smoky haze that made Leary's eyes water. Making his way to the leather chair on which Snyder sat, puffing away, Leary hoped he wasn't inhaling too many toxins.

If Snyder was surprised to see him, he hid it well. He blew out a stream of smoke, rested his cigar on the edge of an ashtray, and leaned back in the chair. The old leather creaked.

"How'd you find me here, Detective?"

"Your receptionist."

Snyder smirked. "I don't think so. Danielle knows better than that."

"I told her it was an emergency."

The silver-haired lawyer's smirk only deepened. "She *definitely* knows better than that."

"You're right. She does. But when she opened her calendar to help me make an appointment, I peeked at her computer screen and saw your appointments for this morning."

Snyder cursed under his breath. "I can't talk. I have court in a few hours."

"Yeah, I see you're working really hard to prepare for the hearing."

"Did Jessie send you here to bust my ass?"

"No. She can do that herself. I came here for legal advice." Seeing Snyder perk up, he added, "*Free* legal advice."

The lawyer scowled. "What do you want, Leary? Wait, let me guess. You proposed to Jessie and she wants you to sign a prenup. Smart girl."

Snyder's guess hit a little too close to home. Leary's mind flashed on the engagement ring hiding in a drawer in their apartment. He forced away the thought. "I want to know more about medical malpractice."

Snyder picked up his cigar and puffed thoughtfully. "If you've suffered from the incompetence of some quack, you've come to the right place. I have a team of lawyers specializing in—"

"This is just research. I'm working a case."

"With Jessie?"

"Does that matter?"

Snyder pointed his cigar at Leary. "You're even less fun than your girlfriend."

Leary sighed. If Jessie could be patient with this clown, then so could he. "The case I'm working involves a doctor—a surgeon —who was the subject of a medical malpractice claim. The complaint alleged lack of informed consent."

Snyder nodded. "Sure. I've used that one plenty of times."

"What does it mean?"

The lawyer laughed. "Before he can slice you up, a doctor is required to give you information—side effects, complications, anything that could affect your decision to move ahead with the treatment. We call it a duty to disclose. For example, let's say a guy needs surgery on his balls. In his zeal to save his patient, the doc neglects to mention that this surgery can sometimes result in a limp dick. Guy does the surgery, and sure enough, finds that he can no longer get it up. Now he's got a claim against the doctor—maybe for hundreds of thousands of dollars. The beauty of it is that the doctor doesn't even have to screw up the procedure. He can perform the surgery flawlessly—more carefully, more diligently, and more safely than any doctor has ever performed it in the history of medicine—but if he didn't warn the guy about that complication, he's liable. First question I ask every potential med mal client—did the doctor warn you this could happen?"

Leary considered Snyder's explanation. On the one hand, it sounded like a *gotcha*, and didn't seem particularly fair to the doctor, but on the other hand, he wouldn't want to be rolled into an operating room without knowing the risks. In some ways, the rule reminded him of the Miranda warnings—*you have the right to remain silent*—viewed by cops as a loophole, but, in the bigger picture, a necessary protection against abuse by the state.

"How would you prove the patient wasn't warned? Isn't that proving a negative?"

Snyder shrugged. "Sure, but this is civil practice, not criminal. I don't need to prove anything beyond a reasonable doubt, just tell the client's story."

"What if the client lies?"

"What if?" Snyder laughed. "Happens all the time. That's why doctor's offices and hospitals make you sign forms."

"The form is evidence of informed consent?" Leary said.

"Sometimes. It depends. The rules are interpreted in favor of the patient. I've defeated forms before."

"So it's basically the patient's word against the doctor's."

"Right. And most times, the insurance company will settle rather than roll the dice with a jury."

Leary nodded. It made sense. He wondered if that was what had happened to Vicki Briscoe.

"Could a doctor lose his or her license for failing to get informed consent?"

Snyder puffed on his cigar, seeming to think about the question. "Possibly. It would be unusual though. I guess if the State Board of Medicine already had it in for someone and was looking for an excuse, they could cite the incident as unprofessional conduct, maybe even fraud or misrepresentation, unethical behavior, and use that to justify taking the guy's license. Why are you asking me all these questions, Leary? Why would the DA's Office care about med mal law?"

"I'm not at liberty to say."

"Surprise, surprise."

This time, Leary smirked. "Thanks for your help, Noah."

Unlike Snyder's hypothetical patient, the plaintiff that Kelly Lee had represented in the medical malpractice case against Vicki Briscoe had not suffered any damage to his private parts. According to the information Briscoe had given Jessie, the case involved complications from surgery to repair a ruptured biceps tendon.

Briscoe had given Jessie the patient's name and address. Leary wasn't sure if that was a HIPAA violation—did doctor-patient privacy laws apply after the patient sued the doctor?—and it wasn't Leary's job to know. The guy's name was Alphonse Fulmer. Leary staked out his apartment in Society Hill, and, when he left, followed him to a local bar.

First a cigar lounge, and then a bar, all before noon. Just a day in the life of a DA's Office detective.

Fulmer walked with a pronounced limp, which made Leary question his own knowledge of anatomy terms. The biceps tendon was in the arm, right? When the guy slid onto a bar stool and greeted the bartender with a wave, both of his arms seemed to be working fine.

Other than Fulmer, the bar was empty. Leary chose a seat two stools away from him.

The bartender brought Fulmer his drink without bothering to take an order, which told Leary he was a regular. The drink was bottom shelf gin, straight, before noon, which told Leary the man probably had a drinking problem.

Leary ordered a beer. He drank it slowly, biding his time as Fulmer worked his way through several fresh gins. He hoped the alcohol would make the man more receptive to conversation with a stranger. Waiting also gave Leary a chance to get a good look at the man. He was short, with thinning gray hair that looked like it hadn't been washed in days. His body was skinny, and the wrinkled shirt and old, dirty jeans he wore seemed to hang off his frame. He stared at nothing. His movements were languid, sleepy.

Leary picked up his beer and moved to the stool next to him. "I guess you like gin. Always been a beer man myself."

"I don't even taste it anymore." Fulmer stared down at his now empty glass, then turned his watery gaze on Leary. His pupils were constricted. He scratched at his neck, where the skin was red and irritated.

Leary's cop brain catalogued these details. The pinpoint pupils, itchy skin, slow breathing, and skinny body were all signs of opiate abuse.

"You hurt your leg?" Leary said.

Fulmer shrugged. "Nothing serious."

Leary nodded. "I ask because I have surgery tomorrow. On my back. I'm pretty nervous about it."

Fulmer turned slightly on his stool. For the first time, the man's eyes seemed to show interest. "What's wrong with it?"

"I get back pain a lot. Doc thinks some surgery will make it better."

Fulmer seemed to hesitate for a second, then said, "I'd think twice about that surgery, if I were you."

"Bad experience?"

"You see this arm?" Fulmer patted his right arm. "Looks normal, but there's nerve damage you can't see. I need to take five Vicodins a day just to stand it."

"How'd that happen?"

"That's what I'm trying to tell you. Surgery."

"You had surgery that went wrong?"

The bartender refilled Fulmer's drink. He emptied the glass into his mouth. "What the doctors call a *complication*. You know what the complications are for your surgery?"

"I'm not sure."

"You better find out." He studied his arm. "Actually, I take that back. Don't find out. That way, anything bad happens, you can sue."

"Is that what you did?"

Fulmer nodded slowly. "You bet I did. Go to the doctor with a hurt tendon, come out with permanent nerve damage? You bet I sued."

"Your doctor didn't warn you that the procedure might cause nerve damage?"

Fulmer opened his mouth to answer, then paused. His eyes narrowed. Leary realized he'd slipped up, used words that were too specific. He'd made Fulmer suspicious.

To the bartender, Fulmer said, "Give me the tab, Jim."

"Settling up already?" The bartender looked surprised, but brought over the check. Fulmer paid in cash, from a thick wad of bills.

Fulmer lowered himself carefully from the stool and started to limp away.

"Did the nerve damage affect your leg?" Leary said.

Fulmer stopped. "You ask a lot of questions."

"Sorry. I'm just nervous about my surgery, especially after what you told me happened to you."

Fulmer shook his head and limped out of the bar without looking back.

"Poor guy," the bartender—Jim—said from behind Leary.

Leary turned to him. "Yeah. Sad story."

"You don't know the half of it." Jim cleared Fulmer's glass and wiped down the bar with a rag. "The surgery messed up his arm, like he told you, but then he got a lawyer. He got a big payout from the hospital's insurance company—not enough to make up for the chronic pain he'll suffer for the rest of his life, but it's better to suffer with money than without it, right?"

Leary nodded. "I agree with that."

"But bad luck always seems to follow that guy. No sooner did he get the money, someone attacks him on the street, breaks his leg. Can you imagine?"

"He was attacked?"

The bartender nodded grimly. "Some thug, jumped off a motorcycle, hit Al's leg with a bat, then got back on his bike and sped away. You want another beer?"

"No thanks." The word *motorcycle* echoed in Leary's mind. "I need to get going."

Leary's phone vibrated in his pocket. He pulled it out and recognized the name on the screen as his contact at the City Hall courthouse.

Leary said, "You have something for me on Judge—"

"Not on the phone. Let's meet. Talk in person."

"Where?"

"Same place we met last time."

The call disconnected before Leary could ask where that

was. It had been years since he'd seen his friend—back when he was still a homicide detective. He let out a curse.

"Bad news?" the bartender asked amiably.

"No, I just—" Then it came to him, the location of their previous rendezvous. *Penn's Landing.* "I need to go."

"Have a good one."

33

LEARY WALKED along the Penn's Landing waterfront. Around him, people enjoyed the restaurants and shops and arcades. Sunlight sparkled pleasantly on the Delaware River. He wished he could relax and enjoy it, but his mind kept flashing on Alphonse Fulmer—the man with the pinprick pupils and gin-tainted breath—and his limp.

It seemed likely that Fulmer's claim about not receiving informed consent before the operation on his ruptured biceps tendon was bogus—cooked up by Kelly Lee as an easy win with the hospital's insurance company, just like Noah Snyder had explained. He'd interviewed enough witnesses, questioned enough suspects, to know when someone was hiding something. That meant Vicki Briscoe really had been wronged. The medical malpractice claim against her had been fabricated. A lawyer's trick.

And the revocation of Briscoe's medical license? Leary remembered Noah Snyder's comments on that, too. He'd said the medical board might use the medical malpractice claim as a pretext for revoking a license, if the board was already looking for a reason. Vicki Briscoe was the daughter of a well-known criminal, a gang leader. Leary had no trouble imagining the backroom political discussions at the State Board of Medicine, old white men steeped in tradition and propriety. *Can we get rid of her? She doesn't belong here.*

He grimaced. But what really bothered him was the limp. The bartender had told him that Fulmer had been attacked by a man on a motorcycle. Ray Briscoe was the leader of the Dark Hounds Motorcycle Club. Coincidence? He didn't think so. Fulmer's claim ruined Vicki Briscoe's career, so her father—or maybe Briscoe herself—arranged for some revenge in the form of a baseball bat to the knee.

And now Jessie was spending time with this woman.

She can take care of herself. Leary mouthed the words, but he wasn't sure he believed them—not in this scenario. *Briscoe has no reason to want to hurt her.* That sounded better. But was it true? Hadn't Jessie mentioned prosecuting Briscoe's boyfriend?

A voice jerked him back to the moment. "I forgot how lovely Penn's Landing can be." It was Warren Williams.

"Thanks for meeting me on short notice," Leary said.

"Where's your guy?"

"He'll be here. Walk with me."

Warren's breathing sounded heavy, and Leary had to slow his pace so the overweight lawyer could keep up. They had not been walking for more than a few minutes when the smell of cigarette smoke invaded Leary's space. He turned to see a middle-aged man. He wore sunglasses and a fedora, and walked briskly with one hand jammed in a pocket of his windbreaker and the other holding a cigarette to his mouth.

"Who's he?" the man said, indicating Warren.

"My boss."

The man nodded but didn't stop walking. "Okay."

"Is this cloak and dagger routine really necessary?" Warren said between labored breaths.

"I don't want to be seen talking to you. The reasons should be obvious." The man hesitated for a second, then added, "And also, I like to get outside. Gives me a chance to smoke."

"I guess you can't do that in the courtrooms of City Hall," Leary said.

The man blew out a plume of smoke. "It's frowned upon."

"Imagine that." Between this cloud and the one in Noah Snyder's cigar club, Leary's throat was starting to feel irritated.

The man turned slightly as they walked. Through the haze of cigarette smoke, his gaze was wary. "Before I tell you anything, I want to know why you're asking about Dax."

Leary started to answer, but Warren touched his arm, stopping him. "Let's just say I have an interest," Warren said.

"You're planning to tangle with her?"

"She's tangling with me. I don't think I have a choice."

The man nodded. "This judge is dirty. Not just ethically challenged—most of them are that—but this one is on the take. Been accepting gifts from litigants and other interested parties for years."

Warren seemed to take this news in stride, and Leary wondered just how common it was. "Risky. How is she getting away with it?"

"Friends in high places, mostly. People willing to look the other way. And money. Where political expediency doesn't cover her, she just spreads the wealth. The usual facilitators."

"Did she take any bribes in connection with the Rowland case?" Leary said. Warren shot him a warning look, but said nothing.

The man nodded. "As a matter of fact, she did."

Leary felt his stomach drop. Right now, Jessie was pulling out all the stops to prepare for a hearing Judge Dax had set for 2 PM. But if the judge had taken a bribe from Boffo Products

Corporation, then Jessie didn't have a chance. Dax was going to throw out the case.

"Please tell me you brought us evidence," Leary said.

The man patted the bag slung over his shoulder. "Come on, Leary. Have I ever let you down?"

"Give it to me." Warren stopped walking and held out a hand. The man didn't move.

"Giving you what's in this bag could be very dangerous for me."

"The DA's Office will protect you."

The man snorted a laugh, then coughed. To Leary, he said, "This guy serious?"

Leary had been dealing with the man off and on for years, and believed he had established that his word was solid. Still, this request was the first time he'd really tested the strength of the relationship. "If you give us what we need, we'll make sure Dax won't be a threat to you."

"You're going to take her down?"

Leary glanced at Warren, who gave a curt nod. "Yes," Leary said.

The man flicked his cigarette to the ground and stomped it out. "I have a friend, needs a little help."

"You're joking," Warren said, but Leary hushed him.

"What can we do for your friend?" Leary said.

"He was arrested for drunk driving. Can you make it go away?"

"Yes," Leary said. "Right, Warren?"

Warren grumbled a reply.

"You know I'm good for it," Leary said.

"That I do," the man agreed. He opened his bag, withdrew a manila folder, and passed it to Leary. "You better handle her decisively. She slips the net, all of our careers are finished."

"Understood," Leary said.

The man turned and walked away, leaving Leary with Warren. The lawyer looked disgusted. "The DA's Office isn't in the business of doing personal favors, Leary."

"You're really saying that with a straight face?"

Warren sighed. "Fine. I just hope his friend doesn't wind up running over some kid the next time he drives home drunk from a bar. I don't need that on my conscience."

Leary held up the folder. "Right now, this is what matters. Jessie has a hearing before Judge Dax in a few hours. We need to move quickly."

34

JESSIE SQUIRMED ON AN UNCOMFORTABLE, pew-like seat. It had been a long time since she had felt like an outsider in a courtroom, but that's exactly how she felt now. Part of this feeling stemmed from the fact that this courtroom was in City Hall, rather than her familiar stomping grounds of the Criminal Justice Center. Part of it was that she sat in the gallery with the other spectators, rather than at counsel's table as a participant. (Noah Snyder sat with the Rowlands at the plaintiffs' table, and Douglas Shaw sat at a defense's table so packed with lawyers they'd barely been able to squeeze in enough chairs.) But the greatest source of her unease was the feeling that she didn't understand the rules here, that Judge Dax, Noah Snyder, and Shaw's legal team were playing a game no one had shown her the manual for, and which had little to do with the facts of the case or the legal research she'd spent the first half of her day working on. And there was nothing she could do but watch.

Judge Dax opened the proceedings. They were assembled here this afternoon for a motion hearing, which meant the lawyers for each side would try to persuade the judge to rule in their favor on the two motions before the court—the plaintiff's motion to certify a class and the defense's motion for summary judgment. Snyder was still riffling through the document Jessie had prepared for him. It was a legal roadmap of the arguments she hoped would carry the day for the Rowlands and other victims of Boffo's recklessness. They had also filed her hastily prepared reply brief.

The lawyers at the defense table sat stone-faced with their hands clasped in front of them on the tabletop. They looked calm and prepared. And confident. Either they were great actors, or they knew something Jessie didn't, since as far as she'd been able to determine, the law was on the Rowlands' side.

"I've considered your motions," Judge Dax said, "and before I rule, I will hear arguments. Mr. Snyder?"

Snyder stood up. He flashed the judge his trademark, rakish smile, but Dax only regarded him coldly. Snyder faltered, but only for a second. Then he smiled again and glanced at the document in his hands.

"Your Honor, as you know, my clients seek certification as a class for purposes of the Commonwealth's class action statute. Courts have consistently held that Pennsylvania's class certification rules are to be applied liberally. See, uh, *Inn Braun v. Wal-Mart Stores Inc.*, a Pennsylvania Supreme Court decision—"

One of Boffo's lawyers stood up. "Your Honor, I don't believe that case was cited in plaintiffs' brief."

Snyder shot the man an annoyed look. "It was cited in our reply brief."

"A reply brief that was filed literally minutes before this hearing, Your Honor."

Snyder looked at the judge with a pained expression. "As you know, the plaintiffs in this case substituted counsel between the filing of the motion and this hearing, as a consequence of the death of their original attorney. But I can assure you that we provided as much notice as was possible given the circumstances. If Your Honor would prefer to postpone this hearing to give the defense additional time to review the reply brief, we would not object to that."

"That won't be necessary," Dax said. "Go on."

"Thank you, Your Honor." Snyder glanced again at his document. "As I was saying, the Pennsylvania Supreme Court upheld a jury verdict in favor of the class action plaintiffs in that case. I would also point your attention to another decision, *Weinberg v. Sun Co.*, where the court held that a class action method does not need to be superior to alternative modes of suit."

He flipped a page, and Jessie cringed inwardly as she watched him quickly read what she'd prepared for him. She hoped he wasn't reading this for the first time.

"Your Honor," he went on, "for a suit to proceed as a class action, Rule 1702 only requires five criteria to be met. It is not intended as a demanding standard. Therefore, it is our position that class certification should be granted here."

"Your Honor," another of Shaw's lawyers said, "the burden of proving those elements is on the moving party. The plaintiffs here have not shown them."

"Not true," Snyder said. He flipped more pages. "Let's see. First element. Right. The class must be so numerous that joinder of all members is impracticable. That's an easy one. How many of these deadly toys did the defendants foist upon the unsuspecting public? Thousands? Tens of thousands? More? The exact number doesn't really matter because...." He flipped more pages, hurriedly looking for Jessie's argument to back up his comment. Watching him, she gritted her teeth. Then he found it and read, "'The class representative need not plead or prove the number of class members so long as she is able to define the class with some precision and affords the court with sufficient indicia that more members exist than it would be practicable to join.' *Bam*."

"*Bam?* Hardly." Shaw's lawyer smirked. "To date, the Rowlands are the only people alleging an injury from my client's products."

"Oh, come on," Snyder said. "The toy was a bestseller last Christmas."

"There's also the element of commonality, Your Honor," Shaw's lawyer said. "Questions of fact must be common to the class. Thousands of toys may have been sold, but that doesn't mean every purchaser is in the same factual position. The common question of fact means the facts must be substantially the same so that proof as to one claimant would be proof as to all. That's from *Allegheny County Housing Auth. v. Berry*, which, by the way, *was* cited in the defense's brief."

"That's a very narrow reading of the law," Snyder said. The sound of flipping pages filled the courtroom. "Just give me a second here."

Judge Dax sighed and shook her left arm so that her judicial robe fell away from her watch. She read the time, then glared out at the courtroom. "I've heard enough. Although I am certainly sympathetic to the plaintiffs in this action, I do not feel that a class action is appropriate here. For that reason, I am denying the motion to certify a class—"

Noise erupted from the plaintiffs' table as Ken and Deanna Rowland, looking angry and shocked, peppered Snyder with questions about how this could happen. Across the aisle, Douglas Shaw smiled knowingly. Jessie noticed that he carefully avoided eye contact with the judge.

Almost as if....

Jessie bit her lip. Had Shaw and his lawyers known all along that Dax would rule in their favor? Was Dax in Shaw's pocket? If so, the Rowlands didn't have a chance. This ruling was only the beginning. Next, Judge Dax would consider the defense's motion for summary judgment, and she would grant it, throwing out the Rowlands' case forever.

The courtroom doors opened with a bang. Jessie watched as uniformed police officers streamed into the courtroom, apparently not concerned that their entrance was disrupting a legal proceeding. Behind them, Warren Williams and Mark Leary followed. Jessie's breath stopped. *What the hell were they doing here?*

Snyder shot her a questioning look. All she could do was shake her head.

The bailiff started to object, then realized what he was seeing and shut up. Judge Dax rose slightly from the bench. "What is the meaning of this?" Her voice was as imperious as ever, but Jessie noticed the way her gaze fell on Warren. She went pale.

"Cynthia Dax," one of the cops intoned, "you are under arrest."

Jessie could barely hear the rest of the litany as an uproar in the courtroom drowned out the *Miranda* warnings. But she did see one of the cops lock handcuffs around the judge's wrists like the criminal she was.

Jessie joined Warren and Leary as the cops led Judge Dax toward the courtroom doors. Jessie realized too late that their paths were going to intersect. She stood rooted in place with Warren and Leary. Dax walked straight toward them.

"Well, look who's here. The whole team. Shouldn't you people be prosecuting homicides, instead of harassing a judge?"

Jessie pressed her lips together. Warren and Leary also remained silent in the face of the woman's hostility.

The cops tried to push the judge forward, but she jerked out of their grasp. "If my career is over, I'll make sure yours are, too. That's a promise."

"No, that's a threat," Warren said, "and one I highly doubt

you'll be able to carry through. I think you'll find that you don't have as many highly placed friends as you thought. Those kinds of friends tend to disappear when the handcuffs come out."

"We'll see," Dax said.

"Ending our careers won't help you anyway," Jessie said.

"Revenge is its own reward."

The cops jerked Dax forward, and this time the judge went willingly. Jessie watched them disappear through the courtroom doors.

Jessie sense Warren looking at her. She turned and saw his serious expression. "Judge Dax is out of the picture now, Jessie. The Rowlands will get a new judge, and you better believe, after this, he or she will handle the case strictly by the book. Your job here is done. It's time to let this go."

"Warren's right," Leary said.

Jessie was grateful for their help, but she wasn't ready to let it go yet. "What about Kelly? If Douglas Shaw had her killed—"

"I gave you a chance to find evidence," Warren said. "Did you?"

"No, but...."

"But what?"

"Let me talk to Judge Dax. Now that she's under arrest, she'll be sure to turn against Douglas Shaw to reduce her own sentence. Maybe she knows something about Kelly's accident."

"That sounds like a long shot," Warren said.

"No harm in trying, though," Leary said. Jessie was glad for his support.

Warren seemed to consider. "Fine. Talk to her. But this is it, Jessie. One way or the other, this is the end of your involvement in the Kelly Lee matter. Agreed?"

With some reluctance, she nodded. "Agreed."

35

AT THE POLICE STATION, Jessie watched Cynthia Dax through the one-way mirror of the interrogation room wall.

Dax had managed to reach her lawyer—Micah Burnside—en route to the police station, and the man had arrived only minutes after Dax was booked. Now he rested a hand reassuringly on Dax's arm and spoke to her in what looked like a quiet, measured tone.

Burnside was a top-tier criminal defense attorney who'd once been known for his prowess defending murderers, but, in his middle age, had fallen into the easy and comfortable practice of rescuing the irresponsible children of the rich and powerful from drunk and disorderly conduct and other embarrassing charges. Apparently, he also helped politicians get out of trouble.

His presence seemed to calm his client. Dax still looked angry, but the fear that had been evident on her face when the cops had led her out of her courtroom in handcuffs seemed to be gone now. Jessie needed to change that, and quickly.

"I'm going to talk to them."

The cop standing at her side, a detective named Leo

Ferguson who specialized in corruption investigations, looked like he might object. But when he turned to speak, something in her expression must have stopped him. "Okay."

Jessie entered the interrogation room. "Hello, Micah." She shook the lawyer's hand, then sat down. She did not offer her hand to Dax even though the woman's wrists were no longer shackled. She barely managed a polite, "Judge Dax."

The woman's eyes flared with anger. "I hope you realize you are going to regret this day for the rest of your life."

Burnside squeezed his client's arm. "Cynthia, I know how frustrating this situation must feel, but it would be better if you let me do the talking."

"I'm a judge and a lawyer," Dax snapped at him. "You can trust me not to say anything I shouldn't."

Burnside did not look convinced, but he nodded. "Of course."

Jessie leaned forward. "You may be a judge and a lawyer, but this is a criminal matter. My territory."

Dax sneered. "She's trying to intimidate me," she said to Burnside.

Burnside watched Jessie carefully. "Or bait you into saying something—"

"I get it," Dax cut him off. To Jessie, she said, "I'm going to walk out of here in time for my dinner reservation. You, on the other hand, will walk out of here without a job."

"Do you think so?" Jessie said.

Dax crossed her arms. "I know so. Whatever evidence you think you have—"

"We have an email exchange between you and one of the attorneys for Boffo Products Corporation. We also have financial statements showing the transfer of money from an account held by one of Boffo's subsidiaries to an account you maintain offshore." Working from the materials Leary's contact had provided, Detective Ferguson had built a file with impressive speed.

Dax's lips pressed together. A look of fear touched her features.

"Are you familiar with Section 4701 of the Pennsylvania Criminal Code?" Jessie said. "'*A person is guilty of bribery if he offers, confers or agrees to confer upon another, or solicits, accepts or agrees to accept from another: (1) any pecuniary benefit as consideration for the decision, opinion, recommendation, vote or other exercise of discretion as a public servant, party official or voter by the recipient; (2) any benefit as consideration for the decision, vote, recommendation or other exercise of official discretion by the recipient in a judicial, administrative or legislative proceeding; or (3) any benefit as consideration for a violation of a known legal duty as public servant or party official.*' Sound familiar? That's a third degree felony, Judge Dax."

Burnside cleared his throat loudly. "Remember, you don't have to say anything."

Dax ignored him. Her glare seemed to bore into Jessie. "What does that mean, a third degree felony? Are you saying I could go to prison?"

"Up to seven years, and I'll make sure you serve every minute of it. How old will you be in seven years? What will you have missed out on?"

"I can't go to prison—"

Burnside spoke over his client. "You obviously want something, Jessie, so why don't we cut to the chase?"

"I want Douglas Shaw."

"Let me speak privately with my client."

"Fine." Jessie rose from her chair. "I'll be back in ten minutes."

Jessie left the interrogation room feeling confident. When she returned exactly ten minutes later, she felt even better. Dax had lost what was left of her composure. Her face was drawn, her hair was disheveled, and her eyes looked haunted.

"My client is prepared to testify that Douglas Shaw bribed her to rule in his company's favor in the case of *Rowland v. Boffo Products Corporation*. In exchange, you agree to recommend a fine but no prison time."

"You mean Douglas Shaw's company," Jessie said.

"No." Burnside leaned forward. "I mean Douglas Shaw. He handled the deal himself, and personally met with Cynthia. I trust you understand the value of her testimony now. No prison time."

"I can't agree to that. I can recommend a four year sentence instead of the maximum," Jessie said.

"Two," Burnside said.

Jessie paused. "I can recommend two, but your client's going to need to give me more than a bribery case against Shaw."

Burnside and Dax exchanged a confused look. "More?" Burnside said.

"Did Shaw have Kelly Lee killed?" Jessie said.

Dax's eyes popped wide, as did her lawyer's, and both of their jaws dropped. It would have been comical in different circumstances. Then Burnside laughed quietly to himself. "I was wondering why we were talking to a homicide prosecutor. Now I understand."

"Kelly Lee died in a car accident," Dax said. "Is this some kind of joke?" She looked genuinely incredulous.

"When you met with him, Shaw didn't say anything to you to suggest he may have had a hand in the accident?"

"That's insane—"

"Think," Jessie said. "Try to remember everything he said to you. The way he said it. Looking back, did he ever give you cause to suspect that Kelly Lee's accident might have been intentional?"

Dax shrugged helplessly. "No. I mean, he bribed me. Why would he kill her when he knew he was going to win?"

"Why seek a settlement if he already knew he would win?" Jessie shot back.

"That's easy," Burnside said. "Shaw would require a nondisclosure agreement as part of the settlement. A gag order. Believe me, I work with these rich business owners all the time. Shutting the Rowlands up would be just as valuable—maybe more valuable—than winning at trial."

Jessie nodded. Burnside was right. Bribing the judge made sense. Pushing for a settlement made sense. Killing Kelly Lee didn't.

"Do we have a deal here or not?" Burnside said.

"I'll think about it." Jessie stood up. The room suddenly seemed smaller, the walls closing in. She headed out of the interrogation room, ignoring Burnside's complaints.

"Get what you needed?" Detective Ferguson said.

Jessie didn't answer him. She still had no evidence against Shaw, and if she didn't find some immediately, Warren was going to shut her down. Heading for the exit, she pulled her phone from her bag and called Vicki Briscoe.

"You better be calling me with progress on getting my license reinstated."

Jessie quickly brought her up to speed on Leary's meeting with Alphonse Fulmer. "He's confident Fulmer's story was bogus. Now all we need to do is prove it."

"And you'll be able to do that?"

"Leary is the best detective I know."

"Good."

"But now it's your turn to help me again. Where else did Kelly go? Who else did she talk to?"

Briscoe's sigh carried across the phone line. "Where should I pick you up?"

36

INSIDE A COFFEE SHOP near the police station, Jessie ordered a hot cup of coffee, took it to a table near the window, and warmed herself up while she stared out at the street. The sky was overcast, and the clouds looked ready to dump torrents of rain onto the city. Jessie's focus shifted from the darkening view to her reflection in the glass. She looked defeated.

Had she been wrong this whole time? Had Kelly's death really been exactly what it appeared? An accident?

After Judge Dax's interrogation, she could almost believe that. Douglas Shaw did not have a particularly strong motive to kill the lawyer, and based on everything she'd learned about the man, he didn't strike her as the kind of maniac who would kill without a good motive.

But then she thought about what Emily Graham had told her she'd learned from the lead AID investigator about the accident. Ross Reid had found a brick by the driver's seat, but no brick missing from the wall of the building at the accident site.

It wasn't an accident. You missed something. That's all.

Maybe Shaw had a motive she didn't know about yet. Or maybe Shaw had not orchestrated the accident, but someone else had. As a personal injury lawyer—and one who apparently had no moral compunctions about bending the law—Kelly had probably angered a lot of people.

She'd certainly angered Vicki Briscoe.

Jessie felt a chill. If there was one person who had a motive to kill Kelly, it was Briscoe. Briscoe also had means and opportunity—the classic homicide investigation trifecta. Why had Jessie ruled her out as a suspect? Because she was *too* vicious to have killed Kelly by staging a car accident? Because Jessie believed her when she claimed she would want to kill her slowly, torturing her first?

Suddenly, with Shaw looking less like a killer, Jessie started to question the prudence of driving around the city with Briscoe. She looked at her phone. She'd already called Briscoe, and she was on her way here to pick her up. There was still time to call back, though, make up some excuse so she could think this through....

No. Even if Briscoe was behind the murder—*maybe especially if she was*—Jessie's best chance at finding the killer was to continue Vicki Briscoe's tour of the days leading up to the accident.

Jessie drank two more cups of coffee and watched the sky fill with even more ominous-looking clouds. A clap of thunder sounded in the distance. She was taking the first sip of her fourth cup when Vicki Briscoe called her. "I'm a block away. Meet me outside."

Briscoe's Mercedes pulled to the curb. Jessie got in. Briscoe flashed her a half-smile, then pulled onto the street and drove.

"Looks like it's about to rain," Jessie said.

"What's the next step?"

"You tell me. Where else did Kelly go when you were following her?"

Briscoe navigated through traffic. "No. I meant what's the

next step in getting my medical license back? You said that detective found out Fulmer's claims were lies. Where do we go from there?"

"We don't have actual evidence yet, but we're working on it."

Briscoe took her eyes off the road and gave Jessie an angry look. "You better not be fucking with me."

"I'm not."

"This detective is real?"

"He's real." She almost added that he was her boyfriend but stopped herself. The less personal information she shared with Briscoe, the better.

Briscoe's gaze jumped from Jessie to the road and back. Her expression softened. "You don't look so good."

"It hasn't been a good day."

"No?"

Jessie sighed. "I thought I was closer to proving that Kelly was murdered, and finding her killer, but now ... I don't know. My theory doesn't make as much sense as I thought it did."

"The toy guy?"

"Douglas Shaw. I was so sure he was behind Kelly's death."

Briscoe turned a corner, passing a group of people with umbrellas. "Of course he did it. He had her office and her apartment searched, right? He stole her files."

Had Jessie told Briscoe about the stolen files? She couldn't remember, and now she felt a creeping sense of paranoia. "He was going to win the case Kelly brought against him, and he knew it. It was fixed. He bribed the judge."

Briscoe let out a short, approving laugh. "Smart man. I wish I could go back in time and do that for my case."

"That's not how the legal system is supposed to work, Vicki."

"The legal system *doesn't* work."

"I'm sorry about what happened to you. I'm going to do everything I can to make it right. You have my word on that."

Jessie hesitated, then decided to take a chance. "You think I'm wrong about Shaw? I mean, there was the brick."

"Exactly," Briscoe said. "The brick on the gas pedal."

I definitely never told her about the brick. She'd only learned about it recently herself, from Graham.

Jessie glanced as nonchalantly as possible out the passenger-side window. Could she open the door and jump out? Not without killing herself. Briscoe was driving too fast, racing through the city now that she'd found a path through traffic.

"Can you pull over?" Jessie said.

"Now?"

"I need to use the restroom."

"Can't you hold it in for five minutes? Are you a three-year-old?"

"Okay." Jessie chewed her lip. She didn't want to push too hard and arouse Briscoe's suspicions, but she had to do something. "Let me check in with Leary, see if he's made any more progress on your case."

"Good idea."

Jessie pulled out her phone and called Leary, but when he picked up, she realized she didn't know what to say.

"I'm just calling to check on the Briscoe matter. Have you found anything solid that shows Fulmer was lying about not giving informed consent?"

"You know I've been tied up with other things," Leary said. He paused, then added, "You're calling me in front of her, aren't you?" he said, understanding.

"Alright," she said. Her heartbeat raced as she struggled to think of something to say—something that Briscoe wouldn't notice but that would clue Leary into the danger she was in. Then it came to her—their joke from the other night. "When you have a chance, can you stop by the grocery store?"

"Grocery store?"

"We need tomatoes."

Silence on his end of the line. *Please, please let him understand.*

"Uh, okay, I guess I can stop for groceries."

Vicki Briscoe had pulled her gaze from the street and was watching her. She couldn't risk saying more. "Thanks." She ended the call and put away her phone.

"Tomatoes?" Briscoe said. "I thought this guy was a detective."

"He's also my ... uh ... roommate. I remembered we need—"

"Shit," Briscoe said. Her stare seemed to harden.

Leary might not have understood Jessie's coded language, but apparently Briscoe had.

"Stop the car, Vicki."

"What gave me away?" She seemed to think about it, and then her face lit with understanding. "The brick."

"Let me out of the car."

"I don't think that would be a good idea." Briscoe increased the vehicle's speed.

Jessie studied her determined face. "You killed her? All this time, it was you?"

Briscoe kept her gaze straight ahead, but Jessie could tell she wasn't focused on the road. She was thinking.

"You aimed her car at a wall and used the brick to weigh down the gas pedal?"

Still no response.

"What about her case files?" Jessie said. "Did Shaw's goons steal those? Or was it you?"

Finally, Briscoe turned to face her. "Do you really want to know the answer to that?" Her eyes seemed to search Jessie's.

"I want to know the truth."

She let out a bitter laugh. "That's your problem. I gave you Shaw. I practically giftwrapped him for you. But could you get him arrested for Lee's murder? No. The police have barely even investigated him."

"Shaw didn't kill her." Jessie felt sick. "He didn't even steal her files. That was all you."

"This doesn't need to end badly. We can help each other. Put me on a witness stand. I'll testify against Shaw. I'll say I saw him tampering with Lee's car. And I won't be alone. I can bring a few other witnesses who saw the same thing. Just tell me how many you need."

"Witnesses from your dad's gang?"

"Does it matter?"

"Justice matters. You killed Kelly. You're going to be in the courtroom, alright, but you'll be sitting at the defense table, not the witness stand."

"*Justice?*" Anger flashed in Briscoe's eyes. "Kelly Lee was a scumbag lawyer who cheated insurance companies and ruined careers. Douglas Shaw is a rich bastard who values money more than children's safety and thinks he's above the law. I was a straight-A student my whole life, even though my parents were criminals. I grew up among drug dealers and kidnappers and rapists and killers, and even with all that crap in my life, I still excelled in school, got into college, got into med school. Do you know how hard it is to get into medical school? And it isn't exactly easy once you're there, either. It took everything I had to make it through that program. But I did it. So I could help people. So I could make a difference. And you want to punish *me*?"

"None of that gives you the right to kill."

"I'm giving you one chance here, Jessie."

"No."

Briscoe let out a sigh. Her expression was one of sadness, as if Jessie had let her down. "You know, I was really starting to like you."

"Vicki, if you voluntarily place yourself in police custody and make a full confession—"

Briscoe's hand lashed out and jabbed Jessie with a black device. Pain erupted in Jessie's side and vibrated through her body. Her jaws locked and her body went rigid. *Taser*, she realized. While they had been talking, Vicki must have reached into a pocket.

"Hurts, doesn't it?" Briscoe said. "Good."

Jessie tried to talk, but her mouth refused to cooperate. She couldn't move. The Taser had paralyzed her. She watched helplessly as Briscoe pulled her car into an alleyway and shifted into park. Reaching into the back seat, Briscoe came back with a roll of duct tape and started to bind Jessie's legs and wrists. When Jessie was fully restrained, Briscoe pulled Jessie's phone from her pocket. "I'll take this." Jessie watched her roll down the window and toss out the device.

Then Briscoe shifted the car into reverse, backed out of the alleyway, and resumed their drive.

"You talk about justice," Briscoe said, "but you can't understand justice if you don't understand pain. I'm going to teach you."

The rural landscape was almost pitch black when Briscoe pulled her car onto the winding gravel road of her father's headquarters. Jessie tried not to panic as the car bounced over the uneven surface. The compound of buildings appeared ghostly in the cloud-covered moonlight. She was still bound, duct tape wrapped tightly around her ankles and wrists.

Briscoe had not seen fit to slap tape over her mouth, and the effects of the Taser had worn off, but Jessie remained silent anyway. She wasn't going to beg for her freedom or her life.

Briscoe parked the car next to the largest building—the one Jessie, Leary, and Graham had entered during their first visit to this creepy place, where she'd seen Briscoe operating on one of the gang members. Now, Briscoe pulled a wicked-looking knife from her glove compartment and brandished it in front of Jessie. Jessie did not want to give her the pleasure of seeing her fear, but she could not stop herself from flinching away from the gleaming blade. Briscoe bent down and used the blade to slice apart the duct tape around Jessie's ankles. She left her wrists bound.

"Now you can walk."

Jessie glared at her but did not respond. Briscoe got out of the car, then came around, opened the passenger-side door, and hauled Jessie out by one restrained arm. She gave her a shove and sent her staggering toward the building. "Let's go."

Somewhere close by, a dog growled. Maybe the Rottweiler she'd seen on her first visit?

Thoughts raced through Jessie's mind as Briscoe shoved her inside the building. They were in the middle of nowhere. Amish country. No one knew she was here.

Leary will find me.

Would he though? She'd said the code word, but it hadn't really been a code word. It had been a joke. Would he remember it and realize what it meant? And even if he did, would he figure out *where* she was?

She had to hope so.

37

LEARY STARED at the screen of his phone, which seemed overly bright in the dim lighting of the bar, then put away the device. Across the table from him, Emily Graham arched an eyebrow. "Everything okay?"

"I think so." Leary leaned back against the padded booth seat. On the table in front of him, his and Graham's notes were spread across the old, battered wooden surface. They'd come to this bar so they could discuss the case out of earshot of the DA's Office and the PPD, and although the odor of beer floated temptingly in the air, neither of them was drinking—although they had indulged in a plate of buffalo wings, at Graham's suggestion.

"You look like something's bothering you," Graham said. "That was Jessie who called?"

Leary nodded. The truth was, although her call had been utterly mundane—*pick up tomatoes?*—something was bothering him. He couldn't put his finger on it. "I've been looking into Lee's malpractice suit against Vicki Briscoe. Jessie asked for an update, but I think the question was mostly for Briscoe's benefit. They're together right now, retracing Lee's steps."

"That's it?"

"That and she wants me to pick up some groceries."

"Is that unusual?"

"I don't know." Leary shrugged. "We are living together now, so I guess it makes sense."

"How's that going?"

"Living together?" Leary thought of some of their recent disagreements. Then he remembered their recent kiss, and he smiled. "It's good."

"Glad to hear that." Graham picked up a buffalo wing and managed to eat it without making a total mess of her face and hands—a skill Leary had never developed. He ate, too, with liberal use of his napkin.

When she was done chewing, Graham looked down at the papers on the table. "So we've gone over our notes on Shaw, Lee, and Dax. I see plenty of corruption and other shady crap, but not murder. What are we not seeing?"

Leary shook his head. "A motive, for one thing. I still don't get why Shaw would have Lee killed, when he already had Dax in his pocket. Murders are hard to get away with, and the risks are huge if you get caught. You met Douglas Shaw. Did he strike you as the kind of guy to take unnecessary risks?"

"No."

"Me either."

"What if there's something else Kelly Lee knew about him—some other piece of evidence—that we don't know about?" Graham said.

"Such as?"

"Didn't Jessie say that there might be a criminal element to the case?"

Leary tried to remember his conversations with Jessie. "Yeah, I think you're right. I think she said that Kelly told her she could show that Shaw knew about the danger, but sold the products to children anyway. Jessie said Shaw could go to prison if that was true."

"So maybe that's the missing motive," Graham said. "Shaw takes the risk of having her killed in order to escape criminal prosecution."

Leary took a moment to turn the idea around in his head. "How would he know for sure that killing Lee would accomplish that? He couldn't be sure Kelly hadn't told anyone, or shared the evidence with anyone. I mean, we know she did tell at least *one* person—Jessie."

"Good point." Graham seemed to consider. "Think back to our meeting with Shaw. Did he seem to be hiding anything?"

"He seemed pretty direct."

"But was there anything hidden behind his words?"

Something about the comment brought Jessie back to mind, and made Leary feel uneasy again.

"What's wrong?" Graham said.

Tomatoes. She'd asked him to pick up *tomatoes.*

"Shit!" Leary bolted out of his seat.

———

MINUTES later they were in Leary's car, racing through the rain-slick streets of Philadelphia, heading for Lancaster. Leary couldn't know for sure that he would find Jessie at Ray Briscoe's gang's headquarters in Amish country, but he had a feeling if Jessie had become Briscoe's prisoner, that's where the woman would take her.

"Listen to me! We need backup! This is an emergency—" Graham was on her phone with the local cops in Lancaster County. She was yelling, and not just to be heard over the drumming of rain against the roof of the car. Leary risked a glance at her and saw her frustrated expression and her clenched fist. The local yokels weren't being cooperative. "Yes! I am a detective with the Philadelphia Police Department. You're not hearing what I'm saying!"

Leary's eyes shifted focus to the buildings whipping past. Realizing how fast he was going, he pulled his gaze back to the road.

"Just send some people, damn it!" Graham ended the call. "Jackasses."

"Let me guess. Local law enforcement lost all interest when you mentioned Briscoe's name."

Graham looked furious. "You'd think they'd want to rout those scumbags, if for no other reason than to protect their tourism industry."

"Unless they make more money from their Briscoe industry. A guy like Ray Briscoe knows how to persuade local law enforcement to look the other way."

"More graft," Graham said dully.

"Seems likely."

"So what are we going to do?" Graham's face creased with frustration. "Wait. I think I know someone who can help."

"That's good to hear," Leary said, "because I'm running out of friends. Who do you have in mind?"

"Lorena Torres. She told Jessie to let her know immediately if she found evidence Vicki Briscoe is involved in criminal activity—"

Leary felt all his muscles tighten at once and he almost lost control of the car. "Wait. What?" He shook his head. "Did you just say—"

Graham let out an exasperated sigh. "Yes, Leary. I introduced Jessie to Lorena Torres. Jessie wanted background on Briscoe and Lorena's been a detective in Organized Crime for years—"

"Hold on. *You introduced Jessie to Lorena Torres?*"

"Jessie's in trouble and *this* is what you're focusing on?"

Leary shook his head. "Of course. Right. That's silly." The highway expanded to four lanes as they left the city behind. "Call her."

Graham returned her attention to her phone. "Just don't kill us before we get there," she said.

Leary looked at the speedometer. The needle edged past 80 miles per hour. Probably not a great idea in these conditions, when even with his headlights on and his wipers on full speed, he had to lean over his steering wheel and squint. Rain lashed at the windshield, and the night was so dark that he could barely keep the contours of the highway in sight.

Conditions got even worse when Leary's GPS app led them off the highway and onto a back road. With the rain coming down faster than his wipers could slash away the blur, Leary drove as quickly as he dared. The surrounding area was difficult to make out in the darkness, but Leary sensed they were passing farmland, grain silos, barns. Amish country.

"Look out!" Graham yelled.

A horse and buggy materialized out of the darkness. Leary slammed his foot on the brake and wrenched the wheel sideways. The front of his car narrowly missed the back of the buggy. They went over the side of the road and into muddy grass. The impact bumped his head against the ceiling of his car and rattled his whole body. Pain shot up and down his spine. His heart pounded in his chest.

He looked over at Graham. Her hair was in disarray and her eyes were wide. "Are you okay?" he said.

"Yeah."

Leary twisted the wheel and gunned the engine, trying to shoot the car back onto the road. The wheels spun uselessly in the mud. "Damn it."

"We're stuck?"

"I hope not."

The car was facing away from the road. Through the rain, the headlights illuminated what looked like acres of fields. There was a barn-like building not far from where the car had skidded to a stop. Its doors were open and Leary could see hay and tools in the shadowy interior. He felt like he'd traveled back in time. He was out of his element.

Gazing back at the road, he saw no sign of the horse and buggy. He tried the accelerator again. The engine revved and the wheels spun, but the car didn't move.

"We need traction," Graham said. "I have an idea." She opened the passenger-side door.

"What are you doing?"

"Follow me!" she called over the pounding noise of the rain.

Leary got out of the car and ran after Graham. She was heading for the barn. By the time they reached it, they were both soaked, their shoes covered in mud. At least the barn was dry.

The place was bigger than it had looked from a distance. About the size of a two-car garage. Leary looked around, trying to understand why Graham had led him here.

"If your idea was to make the rest of the trip on horseback, we're out of luck," he said. There were no horses or any other animals in the building.

She squinted at him. "Why would that be my idea?"

"I guess it wouldn't."

Graham pointed at the hay, stacked in neat cubes against one wall of the barn. "That's my idea."

"The hay?"

"Growing up, my family used to visit an uncle who lived in Vermont. He had a cabin set back pretty far from the road. In the winter, I used to help him put down straw in a path from the house to the road. He liked to use straw because it provided traction, wouldn't ruin his lawn, and could be raked up in the spring."

"Okay," Leary said, looking at the hay—or straw, or whatever it was—with renewed interest. "That is a good idea."

They wrestled one of the bales off the pile and got to work. After what seemed like an eternity of working in the rain, they'd created a path from Leary's car to the road.

After a moment's consideration, he grabbed a notebook from his glove compartment, jotted a quick note, and ran to the barn to leave it near what remained of the straw. It had his name and phone number and an offer to pay the owner for what they'd taken.

"Okay," he said when he was back in the car with Graham. "Let's see if this works."

After some initial wheel-spinning, it did work. The tires bit into the straw-covered ground and the car lurched forward. Leary swerved up the slope, maneuvering over the path they had created, and back onto the asphalt, barely keeping control of the steering wheel as it jumped in his hands. The car skidded onto the road and Leary felt the satisfying stability of pavement under his wheels.

"How much time have we lost?" Graham said.

Leary felt the momentary sense of victory deflate. "Too much."

He pressed his foot hard against the accelerator and the car jumped forward. He knew how dangerous this was, knew they'd been lucky the first time, and that the rainy and dark conditions on this isolated rural road could still spell disaster for him. But he didn't care. The only thing that mattered was finding Jessie. He picked up speed, caught up with the horse and buggy, swerved around it, and kept going.

They hurtled along the road for five, ten minutes without incident. Most people had been smart enough not to go driving in this weather, so the roads were mostly empty. The rain continued to pound down, but the rhythm of the windshield wipers and the drumming of the rain almost lulled Leary into a sense of complacency. He almost missed it when his GPS app told him to turn the car off of the road. Leary tapped his brakes and drifted to the spot where the private road, made of soaking wet gravel, led to Ray Briscoe's property. In the rain and dark, he almost didn't recognize it.

There were buildings set back from the road. A Mercedes sedan was parked in front of one of them. Vicki Briscoe's car? Leary drove close to it, parked, and checked his gun. Graham did the same.

"Ready?" Leary said.

She nodded.

He opened the door and climbed out. Rain washed over his face. He made a visor with his left hand and tried to see, holding his gun in his right hand. There was no one inside the Mercedes, but Leary noticed the raindrops drumming against it turned to steam. The vehicle was warm. It had been used recently.

Then Leary saw a woman walking toward them. In the darkness, it was hard to make out details. Tall, good figure, long hair. Was it Jessie? Or someone else? The woman raised a hand, as if in greeting. He couldn't tell.

"Don't move!" Graham trained her gun on the advancing figure. "Stop or I'll shoot!"

"Emily, no!" Leary pushed her arms down, forcing her gun away from the approaching woman. "We don't know if that's—"

He never finished his sentence. Something struck him hard from behind—a blow to the back of his head that drove him down to his knees in the dirt. At the same time, he heard Graham cry out. He tried to see what or who had hit him, but all he saw was the butt of a gun coming down hard into his face. The rest was blackness.

38

Pain brought Leary back to consciousness. Two men were holding him. He was being half-carried, half-dragged down a hallway. He moved his head, trying to locate Graham. The movement brought another burst of pain.

"I'm here, Mark."

He turned the other way and saw her, flanked by two of her own escorts. Bikers, by the look of them.

Leary recognized the building as the same one they'd entered during their previous visit. They passed closed doors, one of which Leary was pretty sure was the room in which Jessie had seen Briscoe operating. No moans came from it now. The only sounds were the grunts of the men manhandling Graham and him down the hallway.

Leary let his feet drag against the floor. He had no desire to make the job any easier for these thugs. But the men were big and the extra resistance barely slowed them down. They dragged Leary and Graham ten more feet. There, the hallway ended at a sturdy-looking door.

"Let me unlock it." A woman's voice. Leary twisted around and saw Vicki Briscoe striding behind them. She walked past

Leary's escorts, unlocked the door, and opened it. The men gripping Leary thrust him into the darkness. His knees hit the floor hard, sending his head into a spasm of agony in the parts of his skull Briscoe's thugs had hit earlier. He gritted his teeth and willed himself not to pass out again. Graham came tumbling in after him.

A voice in the darkness said, "Who's there?" The voice was angry, charged with nervousness, and unmistakably familiar. *Jessie.*

"Enjoy the reunion," Briscoe said. "I'll be back." A kick sent Leary staggering forward. He fell on his face in the darkness. The door closed behind him and he heard the clunking sounds of the locks engaging.

Graham helped him up to a kneeling position. His eyes began to adjust to the darkness and he saw a figure rush toward them. Jessie's familiar and comforting smell enveloped him. "Jessie, thank God!" He hugged her close to him and kissed her.

"Let me breathe, Leary."

"Are you hurt?"

"Briscoe used a Taser on me. Other than that, I think I'm okay."

"Your wrists are bound."

"Duct tape. I've been trying to loosen it, but Vicki wrapped it pretty tight. Emily, is that you?"

"Of course," Graham's voice said from the darkness next to Leary. "You think I'd miss this?"

"Hell of a party," Jessie agreed.

Leary was glad they could make light of the situation, but he couldn't. His hands moved over Jessie's body, searching for wounds. Only when he was satisfied that she was in one piece, did he reluctantly let her go.

"What about you, Leary?" Jessie said. "Are you injured?"

Leary tried to remember the cause of the blinding pain in

his head. One of the bikers had slammed the butt of a gun into his forehead. And seconds before that, someone had hit him in the back of his head, probably with the same gun. It was a miracle his skull hadn't opened like an egg, and he continued to feel sensations of imbalance, nausea, and immense pain. "I'm fine."

"We need to get out of here," Jessie said.

"Why do I doubt Vicki left us a key?" Graham said.

"As far as I can tell this room is empty," Jessie said. "Just four walls and a ceiling, and the one door, which seems securely locked. No windows. No furniture."

"That doesn't give us much to work with," Leary said.

"I'm sorry," Jessie said.

"Don't be sorry," Leary said. "We're going to get out of here."

"We're here because of my stupidity."

"If there's one thing you're not, it's stupid."

"I agree with that," Graham said. "So stop using your brain to feel bad about yourself and start using it to think of a plan."

"I've *been* thinking," Jessie said, "and there's no way out."

"We don't need to escape," Graham said. "We only need to survive long enough for Lorena Torres and her unit to get here. I called them while Leary and I were driving here."

Leary ran a hand through his hair and sighed. "Jessie, as long as we're stuck here for a little bit, and given that there is a certain degree of possibility—very small—that we might not make it out, there's something I want to say to you."

He strained to see Jessie in the darkness, but her face was only a light blur in the gloom, unreadable.

She said, "Okay...."

He licked his lips, suddenly unable to continue. Graham thumped him hard on the back. "Just ask her already!"

"I don't have ... well ... everything with me right now that I need to do this the right way, but what the hell." He knelt on one knee and took her bound hands in his. "Jessica Black, will you marry me?"

"Leary—"

The sound of locks disengaging interrupted them. Leary spun toward the door. It opened, and two figures stood silhouetted in the light from the hallway. Both of them were female. At the same moment, the room lit up with light as someone hit a light switch on the other side of the door. Leary blinked against the sudden glare. Through squinting eyes, he saw Briscoe and a second woman, battered looking, with bruises and blood on her face and wearing tattered rags. Her hair was a disheveled mess. Briscoe shoved her into the room.

"Thought you might like to reconnect with an old friend," Briscoe said. Her voice was full of scorn.

Leary blinked rapidly, almost unable to believe his eyes. The woman was Kelly Lee.

She was alive.

39

VICKI BRISCOE SAT on the porch outside the main building of her father's compound. The porch had a roof, and she leaned back, closed her eyes, and listened to the sound of rain drumming against it. It was a soothing sound, a sound that brought back childhood memories and felt as comfortable as a warm blanket. But she was not warm. It was cold on the porch, and the comforting sound was an illusion.

She opened her eyes and pulled her coat tighter around her body. Now was not the time to allow herself to be lulled into a sense of complacency. Things were accelerating now, much more quickly and in a different direction than she had intended. She knew she needed to think while she still had the opportunity to think. She needed to make decisions and plan ahead now, before a sense of urgency overwhelmed her.

She heard the sound of the screen door open and slam behind her, but she did not turn around. The familiar odor of her father's cigar smoke reached her before the man lowered himself into a chair next to her. She glanced at him, saw the tip of his cigar burn bright red in the darkness. He took the cigar from his mouth and offered her the half smile she'd become so familiar with over the years.

"You want one?"

"You know I don't smoke those things. They can give you mouth cancer, among other negative health effects."

Her father chuckled. "Listen to the doctor."

He frowned the second after the words left his mouth, and she sensed his sudden awkwardness. Her father might be a violent man—a man with his own brand of morals, if you could even call them that—but his love for her was genuine and she knew he worried about causing her even a second's worth of pain.

"Relax, Dad. You can still call me a doctor. I'm not going to break down in tears."

"I know that. Not my daughter."

"Fuck no." Vicki looked away from him. She certainly had broken down in tears—Ray Briscoe's daughter or not—and more than once. When she'd received notice of the lawsuit. When she'd lost her license to practice medicine. She was tough. Her father had raised her to be tough. But she was still a human being—much more so than he was. She believed her father was a sociopath, or, at least, that he had strong socio-pathic tendencies. She wasn't like him. She experienced the full range of human emotions. *Feelings.* Her father would consider this a weakness, and to appease him, she'd spent her life pretending not to experience feelings. Pretending to be him. But she wasn't a sociopath.

A psychopath, maybe, but not a sociopath.

He reclined in the darkness, puffing his cigar. Eventually, he took it from his mouth with a contented sigh. "You gonna tell me who our guests are?"

"You really want to know?"

"I asked, didn't I?"

Vicki hugged herself tighter. "The same ones who came here before."

"The DA and those cops? Jesus Christ, Vicki." Her father took a long pull on his cigar, then blew the smoke out into the night.

"They were too close to finding out the truth about Kelly Lee. I didn't know what else to do."

"You could have asked me."

"Is that what you want? Me running to you every time I have a problem?"

"Actually, yes." Her father sighed. "If you think I wouldn't want that, then I must have gone wrong somewhere raising you."

"If the PPD finds out we have them, they're going to come down on us hard. I'm sorry, Dad."

Her father did not look overly concerned. "I'm not worried about the PPD. We can handle them, like we always have."

He did not elaborate, but Vicki knew enough about the family business to understand what he meant. *Graft, violence, extortion.* "I still have time to finish what I started," she said. "After that, I won't cause any more trouble for you and the Hounds."

"You're no trouble sweetheart." His gaze held some warmth, but only for a space of seconds. "You're not going to finish anything, though. Too dangerous now." He clamped his cigar in his teeth, leaned forward, and pulled something out of his back pocket. He passed it to her. A passport. Flipping it open, she saw her own photograph and someone else's name.

"Dad—"

"The rest of the package is in the house," he said. "In the safe. I'll take care of our guests. You leave tonight. Start fresh somewhere else. Didn't you always admire the beaches of Colombia?"

"I'm not leaving tonight."

His eyes narrowed. They stared at each other as rain continued to pound the roof above them and soak the tall grass surrounding the building. In the distance, she could hear the sounds of his men moving around. Hardened criminals, but not one of them tough enough to stand up to Ray Briscoe. Was she?

She could feel the anger radiating from him. "I didn't raise a stupid bitch."

"That's right. You didn't."

"The smart move is to disappear."

"Yes, at the end. But I'm not there yet."

"The end of what?"

"You know what," she said.

"Where's the upside? It's all risk, no reward."

"For me, it's a reward."

Her father held her gaze for a long moment. She felt her insides go cold and had to struggle not to look away from that stare. Then, after a seeming eternity, he let out a sigh and rose from his chair. "We don't see eye to eye on this one, sweetheart. But you know I'm always on your side."

Until you're not. "I know, Dad. Thanks." But he had already left her. She sat alone outside for a few more minutes, listening to the rain, looking at the fake passport in her lap.

Her father was right. And she would leave. But not before she extracted her pound of flesh.

Literally.

40

"KELLY?" In the darkness of the windowless room, Jessie stared in shock. After almost a week of searching for this woman's killer, her brain rebelled at the idea that she had been alive the whole time.

Kelly stared back at her, but there was no look of recognition in the lawyer's eyes. She looked distant. Absent.

"Kelly, it's me. Jessie."

Kelly said nothing, but her body started to shake uncontrollably. Jessie could hear the rapid pumping of her lungs. Almost hyperventilating.

She tried again. "Kelly? I thought you were dead. Can you tell me what happened?"

No response.

How was this possible? "You were in a car accident. The ME identified you. How—" Squinting in the darkness, Jessie saw the amputations. Several fingers missing from each of Kelly's hands. A chunk of flesh from her right arm. Possibly part of one of her feet, which appeared to be bandaged and bloodied. The driver's body had been found in pieces. The ME's identification had been based on fingerprints.

My God.

Jessie felt a threat of vomit in her guts. Bruises covered Kelly's body, along with dried blood, and stitches where she'd been opened and then sewn up.

Graham's voice from somewhere else in the dark room: "She must be in shock."

Jessie heard Graham and Leary moving around. She supposed they were searching the room for an escape route, a weapon, anything. She already knew they would find nothing.

"Kelly." She tried to penetrate the woman's vacant stare. "We need to get out of here. Is there anything you can tell us?"

Kelly's lips moved. Jessie couldn't hear her. She leaned closer, almost losing her balance with her wrists bound in front of her.

"What did you say, Kelly?"

"Crazy." Kelly's voice was barely a whisper. "She's crazy."

Jessie touched the woman's hand and gave it a reassuring squeeze. "We're going to get you out of here, Kelly."

"They took me. They came into my apartment at night and took me. Vicki Briscoe and ... some men. She's crazy. There's a room. She takes me there and...."

The door opened. Kelly curled up into a ball and started sobbing. Jessie stared at the rectangle of light that was the doorway and the three dark figures framed within it. She recognized Vicki Briscoe's now-familiar shape. The woman appeared to be flanked by two tall and powerful-looking men. The three of them advanced into the room. Kelly's sobs turned into a keening wail as the footfalls echoed in the room and the three visitors surrounded them.

Jessie braced herself for a fight, but against three people who were probably armed, and with her wrists tied, she didn't know what she could do. Headbutt someone? If it came to that, maybe.

She'd seen movies where someone broke an assailant's nose by ramming it with a forehead.

From the corner of her eye, she saw Leary tense up. Graham, standing in another corner of the room, also turned to face the intruders. Both of them were better fighters than Jessie was, and their wrists weren't bound. But they were unarmed.

Briscoe walked past Kelly and stopped in front of Jessie. She grabbed Jessie roughly by the arm and yanked her to her feet, then toward the door. "Time to see what your pain tolerance is, prosecutor."

Leary charged at them. The two men with Briscoe blocked him, one of them grabbing him in a bear hug from behind and the other one slamming a fist into his belly, doubling him over. Graham headed toward them next.

"No, Emily!" Jessie tried to break out of Briscoe's grip, but she couldn't. She swung her head in Briscoe's direction, trying for the headbutt she'd imagined, but all she managed to do was flail. Briscoe laughed at her. On the floor, Kelly continued to wail.

"Don't touch her!" Leary broke free of the man who was holding him and punched the other man with enough force to make him stagger back and drop to one knee. Briscoe cursed and dragged Jessie toward the door. Leary hurtled himself toward them, but the other man grabbed him again and threw him against the wall.

"Let her go!" Graham said.

Briscoe sneered. "Or what?" She tugged at Jessie. "You've got loyal friends. But will it last when they have to choose between you and saving their own skins? We're going to find out after I take a scalpel to your face."

"You obviously don't know anything about loyalty." Jessie wrenched sideways, but she could not get free.

"I know enough about it." Briscoe's grip was like a vise. She was much stronger than she looked. Fueled by insanity, maybe. By mindless rage. Against what? What had Jessie ever done to her? She realized it didn't matter. The world had failed Vicki Briscoe, and the world was going to pay for it.

"That's why you dumped Trevor Galway the second he got in trouble with the law? That's your idea of loyalty?"

Briscoe's face twisted with pain. She glared at Jessie, and drove her fist into her chest. Pain exploded and the breath was forced out of her lungs. Her knees almost gave way, but Briscoe held her up. Her vision swam. She heard nothing but the meaty sounds of the two men beating Leary, the sound of Graham protesting, and the sound of Kelly sobbing on the floor. She struggled to breathe.

"Don't ever say his name again," Briscoe said. "You don't know anything about Trevor and me. You don't know anything about my life."

"I don't want to."

Briscoe threw Jessie through the doorway and into the hall. She followed her over the threshold and kicked the door shut with her boot. It slammed, cutting off the sound of Leary's final, agonized shout.

41

BRISCOE THRUST JESSIE OUTSIDE. She staggered, almost losing her footing. The downpour had ceased, but the grass was still wet and her shoes slid on the slick, spongy surface.

"Keep moving," Briscoe said.

With the woman shoving her every few feet, Jessie crossed a short expanse of damp grass to another building on the compound. The night was dark—almost pitch black—and the air smelled like rain. Somewhere nearby, a dog barked. She stopped at the door and dug in her heels, all too aware that his momentary exposure to fresh air and open sky might be her last.

Briscoe shoved her inside. She faced another dark and cramped interior. A smell hit her with such force that she almost threw up. Panic flooded her system and she elbowed Briscoe, trying to flee. Briscoe gripped her arm painfully.

"This way."

Briscoe marched her down a hallway. The smell intensified. It was like something from the morgue, or a crime scene. Blood and death, and the sweaty stink of fear. Briscoe seemed to be watching Jessie's expression as she thrust her toward a room at the end of the hall.

Briscoe opened the door and thrust Jessie inside a small, square room. The stench of the space seemed to propel itself into her nostrils and mouth. She coughed and gagged, overpowered by it. With her wrists bound in front of her with duct tape, she swayed unsteadily and almost collapsed. She forced herself to stay upright, to stay alert. She needed any advantage she could get. She certainly needed to remain standing.

She blinked to clear her vision. There was an operating table in the middle of the room, but it didn't look like anything you'd see in a hospital, or even like the table she'd seen in the other building.

This table wouldn't even pass muster in a hospital from a hundred years ago, or from a war zone. There was no attempt at sterility, little effort at organization or order. The bed was dark with blood, a collage of dried, crusty stains and fresher, damp puddles, different shades of maroon. Jessie smelled sweat, too, a smell that brought to mind feverish perspiration.

This is where she tortures Kelly.

Beside the operating table was a shelf covered in surgical implements. Scalpels, saws, needles, drills. Unclean, darkly stained. Clumps of something clung to the edges of the blades— skin, she realized with a punch of visceral revulsion. *Flesh.* Jessie shuddered, not wanting to look.

This was where Kelly Lee had spent the last week while everyone thought her dead. Taken into this room, worked on, made to scream and sob and cry as her skin was cut apart and she was stabbed and sliced and drilled.

And now, apparently, it was Jessie's turn.

42

Briscoe's grip tightened around Jessie's arm. "Get on the table. Or I'll put you there."

"Who was the woman in the car?" Jessie said.

"What?"

"The woman whose body was found in Kelly's car, after the accident. Obviously, that wasn't Kelly. Who was it?"

"Do you really care, or are you just trying to postpone what's coming next?"

Jessie tried to remain calm, but the surgical instruments—stained and filthy—drew her gaze. The tools of torture. "A little of both."

Briscoe let out a short, harsh laugh. "She was nobody. Just one of the many people stupid enough to cross my father."

"The councilwoman," Jessie said, remembering what Lorena Torres had said at the diner.

Briscoe's laugh abruptly cut off. "You should be begging for your life. Instead, you're giving me more reasons to kill you? I thought you were smart."

"I try to be." Jessie forced herself to be smart now. To look more closely at the surgical instruments. *Just think of them as tools. How can you use them?*

Only minutes ago, she had been wishing for anything with which to cut the duct tape binding her wrists. Here was a table full of sharp implements.

Tools.

If she could manage to get to one, somehow maneuver it with her bound hands in a way that could cut the tape, then she could get free. Or at least give herself a chance.

Jessie kicked backward with her right leg, trying to connect with Briscoe's shin. The woman dodged her, seemingly without effort, and laughed. "Did they teach you that move in self-defense class?" She punched Jessie hard in the kidneys from behind and Jessie staggered forward, almost crashing into the filthy operating table. She swerved in a different direction and used the momentum to get closer to the table of instruments.

"I thought we established our relative fighting prowess the first time I kicked your ass."

Jessie didn't respond. She inched toward the table of instruments.

"I think I'm going to start with your legs," Briscoe said. "Give you some nice long scars. Maybe slice your Achilles tendons so you can't try to kick me again. Maybe cut off a few toes, make your handsome detective friend eat them like Chicken McNuggets. How does that sound?"

"Leary's more of a Big Mac kind of guy." The closest instrument, a long, extremely sharp-looking scalpel, was almost within reach.

"Get on the table." Jessie braced herself, flexed her hands—which luckily, although bound, had not gone completely numb—and made a quick grab for the scalpel. She got the instrument into her hands and fumbled with it, trying to rotate it so that the blade reached the tape between her wrists. Briscoe watched her with a bemused smile. "Seriously?"

Jessie struggled against rising panic, but she couldn't get the leverage she needed to saw at the tape. Briscoe closed the distance between them and reached for her hands. She was going to take the scalpel from her, and probably inflict a little damage as a punishment. Jessie watched Briscoe's hand come toward her, and a thought flashed into her mind. *Surgeon's hands*, Briscoe had called them, the day she'd panicked at the coffee counter of a University City bookstore. *She said she needed to protect her surgeon's hands.*

Jessie had an idea. She stopped trying to maneuver the scalpel toward the tape. She held it out toward Briscoe and charged toward the woman. Briscoe jumped back, surprised. But she wasn't fast enough to get out of Jessie's way. The blade connected, slashing across Briscoe's right palm. The skin separated into ugly flaps and blood spurted out. Briscoe wheeled away. "My hand!"

Jessie dropped the scalpel and thrust her hands at the rest of the instruments on the table. There was a heavy looking saw— maybe for cutting through bone?—that looked like it might serve her purposes. She placed her wrists over its teeth and started to piston her arms forward and backward. The tape loosened.

"You ruined my hand, you stupid bitch!"

Jessie sawed faster. The tape separated with a snapping sound. Her hands burst apart. She was free.

Briscoe's eyes were filled with rage. She bared her teeth like an animal. Her fist came up fast. She punched Jessie in the throat. Jessie flew backward. She couldn't breathe. Black spots swam in her vision for one second, two seconds, as she watched Briscoe come at her. Finally, she sucked in a huge lungful of air.

Blood streamed from Briscoe's fisted right hand. Jessie threw her own punch, but missed. "Get on the table!"

"Make me."

Briscoe reached for her. It was what Jessie had hoped she would do. When her right fist opened, exposing the slashed palm, Jessie grabbed it and dug her nails into the wound. Briscoe screamed and ripped her hand free.

Jessie saw the scalpel she'd dropped earlier, still on the floor in a small pool of Briscoe's blood. She lunged for it. Briscoe saw what she was doing and tried to beat her to the weapon. Jessie let herself fall to the floor, swept up the scalpel, and rolled onto her back. She let out her own scream and thrust upward. The blade entered Briscoe's chest just as the woman crashed on top of her.

Briscoe's eyes, inches from Jessie's, filled with a look of confusion. She let out a soft, "*Urk*."

Jessie let out a sigh of relief, but in the next instant, Briscoe's eyes brightened again, full of hate. Her hand came up and her fingers wrapped around Jessie's throat.

Jessie felt her airway cut off. She gritted her teeth and forced the blade deeper into Briscoe's chest. Blood flowed down the metal handle and coated Jessie's hands. She pushed harder and felt the steel scrape past the resistance of Briscoe's ribs. It sank into her heart.

Briscoe's eyes went out of focus. Her fingers loosened. Jessie could breathe again. The scalpel slipped out of her grip but stuck in Briscoe's chest. Blood pumped out of the woman, flooding the floor. Jessie breathed heavily, watching the woman on top of her die.

She felt a sickening sensation, but forced herself to roll out from under the body. She was still in danger, and so were Leary, Graham, and Kelly. She got to her knees in the blood and searched Briscoe's clothing. She was looking for two things. She found one of them in the pocket of Briscoe's jeans—a ring of keys. She did not find the second thing she was looking for, which was a phone.

Jessie took the keys. After a second's hesitation, she took one of the other surgical instruments as well—another scalpel. Then she hurried out of the room. There was no one in the hallway. She crept forward until she reached the building's exit.

The night was still chilly and damp, the grass wet beneath her shoes. She could hear men talking in the distance, rough laughter, the clink of bottles. She couldn't see anything in the darkness. She moved forward, slowly and silently, in what she hoped was the direction of the other building. No more than ten feet away, she saw a flash of light as someone lit a cigarette. Her breath caught in her throat. After a moment, she moved forward.

She crept past the smoking man. The main building came into sight. There was no one in front of it. No guards.

Thank God.

With her goal in sight, she moved more quickly. One step. Two steps. With one more sprint she could reach the door....

A low growl stopped her in her tracks. Turning her head, she saw the eyes of the Rottweiler glittering in the darkness not more than six inches away.

She froze and closed her eyes, waiting for the pain of the animal's teeth tearing out her throat. But no pain came. The growl subsided into a husky panting sound.

She opened her eyes. The dog was still watching her, but his gaze didn't seem as menacing. She remembered seeing the animal in the light. An older dog, overweight and placid. Maybe even friendly.

"Shhhhh," she whispered. "It's okay. Good doggie."

The Rottweiler wagged its tail. Jessie let out a breath of relief. She petted the dog on his head, then behind his ear. Then, leaving him behind, she continued her progress toward the biker gang's main building.

The door was not locked. She slipped inside. The front room was empty. She gripped the scalpel tighter, hoping her luck would hold. She went down the hallway, found the room she was looking for, and started trying the keys on Briscoe's ring. The third key fit. She unlocked the door and opened it, stepping into darkness.

A shape came at her and knocked her to the ground. Pain flashed through her body.

43

IN THE DARKNESS, someone tackled Jessie and drove her to the floor. A surprised cry escaped from her throat. She cut it off quickly. The last thing she wanted to do was draw attention.

"It's okay. It's just me." She whispered as loudly as she dared.

The person who had knocked her over was Leary. In the darkness, his eyes looked wide and unbelieving, shiny with tears. His hands searched her body, her face, as if he couldn't believe she was here. He must have imagined her being tortured. He'd been trapped in here with Graham, tending to the wreck that was Kelly, and imagining what was happening to her.

"Mark, I'm okay. I'm okay."

"What did she do to you?" His voice broke. His hands continued to roam. "You're covered in blood."

"Her blood."

"Where is she?" Graham said. Looking past Leary, Jessie could see the detective standing near the wall.

"Dead." Speaking the word sent a tremor through Jessie's body. She had killed the woman. She knew, rationally, that she had had no choice. That Briscoe meant to do her incredible harm. But for some reason, that didn't stop the guilt. It never did.

Leary stared at her, as if having trouble comprehending what she was telling him. "How?"

"I stabbed her in the heart."

"You're sure she's dead?"

Jessie shuddered again. Now tears slid from her own eyes. She nodded. "We need to get out of here before someone finds her body."

"They took my car keys," Leary said.

From the darkness, Graham muttered a curse. Jessie thought she heard Kelly groan as well.

"I have Vicki's keys." Jessie held up the keyring, squinting to see the keys. One of them was attached to a Mercedes key fob.

"When Graham and I got here, we saw a Mercedes parked out front," Leary said. His composure seemed to be quickly returning, and with it, a sense of purpose. He turned to Kelly. She lay curled up in a fetal position. Leary crossed the room and gently touched her shoulder. "Kelly, can you stand up? We need to leave."

Kelly didn't move. Jessie wasn't even sure she'd heard or understood him.

"She's traumatized," Graham said.

"Can you carry her?" Jessie said to Leary.

"I think so. But that means I won't be able to fight if we get surprised on the way out."

"Emily can fight," Jessie said. "And I'm not so defenseless myself."

"I think you proved that tonight," Graham said. Leary looked uncertain.

"We can't leave her here," Jessie said.

"I know." Leary bent down and gathered Kelly into his arms. Her limbs hung limply from her, swaying slightly. Leary grunted as he hefted her up and over one shoulder. "She's heavier than she looks."

Jessie was already on her feet. She gripped the scalpel in one hand and grabbed the doorknob with the other. "It's a straight shot up this hallway to the main room of the building. Then through a door to the outside. Briscoe's car should be right in front."

"Okay," Graham said. "We move fast and quiet, get Kelly into the back seat, get in the car, and go. You ready?"

"Hold on." Leary adjusted the weight he was carrying. Kelly's black hair, disheveled and blood-caked, hung down his back. "Ready."

Jessie started to turn the knob, then paused. She realized they might not make it. She looked back at Leary. "Yes."

"Yes what?"

"Yes, I'll marry you."

A smile spread across his face, bright even in the darkness of the room.

"As novel as it is to watch a proposal in a dungeon," Graham said, "I'd really like to get the hell out of here."

"I love you," Leary said.

"I love you, too. So let's try not to die." Jessie turned the knob and opened the door.

44

JESSIE AND GRAHAM entered the quiet hallway, with Leary a step behind carrying Kelly Lee. There was no sign of the bikers. Not yet, anyway.

They made their way up the hallway as planned, and entered the main room where they'd first met the bikers and Ray Briscoe. There was no one there now. The lights were off and the room was quiet. Jessie opened the door to the outside.

At first, Jessie thought Briscoe's car wasn't there. Her heart slammed in her chest and her mouth went dry. Then her eyes found the vehicle's sleek, black form, almost invisible in the darkness. She led the way and they hurried to the Mercedes. Jessie unlocked it with the key fob. The car emitted a chirp that seemed excruciatingly loud to Jessie. She froze, cringing, waiting for discovery. The dog barked once, but there were no other sounds. Letting out her breath, she opened the rear passenger door.

Graham helped Leary lever Kelly into the back seat. Her body flopped lifelessly across the seats. Leary pushed her legs into the car and closed the door. Then he turned to Jessie. "Always fun when we get to work together."

"Barrel of laughs."

A gun shot rang out. The side of the car punched inward no more than an inch to Leary's right. Jessie realized it was the force of a bullet hitting the vehicle's frame.

"Don't fucking move." A familiar voice, calm but steely.

Ray Briscoe.

"Shit," Graham said.

"Someone find Vicki," Ray Briscoe said. "The rest of you kill these bastards."

Jessie glanced at Graham, then exchanged a look with Leary. The three of them ducked and moved quickly. Jessie could hear other voices now, and boots pounding the wet grass. More gunshots split the quiet of the night. The rear door's window shattered. Jessie crouched by the driver's side door, opened it, and got behind the wheel. Leary got in on the other side. Graham climbed into the back, squeezing next to Kelly. The lawyer lay prone across the back seat, covered in pieces of glass from the exploded window.

"Go!" Leary said.

Jessie stabbed the ignition and shoved her foot down on the gas pedal. The Mercedes leapt forward.

In her haste to swing the car around, she almost lost control. The steering wheel jumped in her hands and the left-hand tires went off the gravel road and into the grass. She righted the vehicle and got it turned in the direction of the main road leading out of the property. Gunshots continued to fire from behind them.

Leary put a reassuring hand on her arm. "Stay calm."

"Kind of hard to stay calm when people are shooting at us." She floored the accelerator and the car rocketed along the narrow gravel road toward the exit of the compound. The gunshots petered out, but a new sound replaced them. *Engines.*

Cars and motorcycles came to life behind them, dozens of head-lights spearing the darkness.

"That's not good," Jessie said.

"Just drive."

"They didn't teach car chases in law school. Maybe I should have let one of you take the wheel."

Graham said, "Well, I wasn't going to say anything at the time, but—" The side view mirror on Jessie's left exploded.

They bounced along the gravel road and swerved from there onto the main road. The members of the Dark Hounds gang pursued them. In the back seat, Kelly whimpered. The bouncing and jostling of the car must have been painful on her wounded and bruised body, but there was no avoiding it. Jessie wished any of them still had their phones. They were on their own out here in the middle of nowhere. Even assuming Torres was on her way, it didn't look like she was going to get here in time. If the bikers caught up with them, Jessie could not even imagine what retribution Ray Briscoe would visit on them for the death of his daughter.

"They're catching up," she said, watching her pursuers in the rearview mirror.

Several of the Dark Hounds peeled off of the road, bounding up a side road that intersected it. *They're going to flank us*, Jessie thought. This area was the Hounds' home turf. They knew the roads around here—the shortcuts and side roads.

"Speed up," Leary said. "I have an idea."

Jessie had already pushed the Mercedes past ninety miles per hour. On the dark, slick road, she was afraid to go faster. "Leary...."

He pointed. "See up ahead, how the road bends? Get there."

She shoved her foot down hard against the pedal. The Mercedes responded with a growl. The miles-per-hour counter rose, exceeding one-hundred. The car whipped around the bend. The night seemed to darken as the headlights behind them disappeared.

"Slow down," Leary said.

"What? Why?"

"Just trust me," he said.

"Do it," Graham said from the back. "I think I know what he's thinking."

Jessie risked a quick glance at the man beside her. He was leaning forward and peering out the windshield, as if searching for something. Jessie let up the pressure on the gas pedal and the car slowed.

"There! See it?"

Jessie had to squint to see what he was pointing at. Then she saw it. A rough path—it looked like muddy straw—running from the other side of the road and down into a field. There was some kind of structure in the field, a shed or a barn, with its doors open. "Yes."

She jerked hard on the steering wheel. The Mercedes half-turned, half-skidded. Even with the windows closed, the smell of burnt rubber filled her nostrils. The front tires bounced off the pavement and onto the straw, then the rear tires followed. The car bumped roughly, throwing Jessie against the steering wheel, and then hard against her seat.

She aimed for the barn, hoping the car would fit. She slammed on the brakes and the car screeched to a halt before just narrowly missing the structure's rear wall. The Mercedes rocked to a hard stop. Jessie caught her breath, then cut the power and extinguished the headlights.

Graham jumped out of the car and ran for the barn doors. As she was pulling them closed, Jessie heard a burst of noise. The sound of vehicles racing past on the road above them. Then it was quiet. She looked at Leary. "It worked. They missed us."

He smiled and nodded. "Now we wait, I guess."

As it turned out, they didn't need to wait long. Only a few minutes passed before the sound of police sirens wailed through the night.

Jessie's breath escaped in a sigh. Leary started to laugh.

"Better late than never," Graham said.

45

RESTAURANT WEEK WAS OVER, but Leary found himself at another fancy restaurant with Jessie and her father. The ambience was subdued and classy, the tables surrounding them occupied by content-looking people chatting happily over their meals. After recent events, Leary found himself envying their normalcy.

Jessie smiled at her father. "This time we promise to stay for the whole meal."

"Don't make promises you might not be able to keep," Harland Black said. "Besides, the last time you bailed on me, you left me enough delicious food to last a week. I wouldn't say no to that happening again."

He gave her a big smile, but Leary, with his trained eye, caught the effort behind it. There was no ignoring the bruises and scratches beneath Jessie's makeup.

Leary remained silent. Under the table, his hand returned incessantly to his pocket, where he traced the hard circle of the engagement ring he'd been holding onto for what felt like an eternity now. Even though he knew what Jessie's answer was going to be, he still felt a tremor of nervousness as the moment approached to ask for real.

Jessie's father put down his menu and gave Leary a wink. "You know what? I think I need to hit the head. See you later, kids." He rose and gave Leary's shoulder a squeeze as he walked past. Leary saw Jessie's face flush red. He was sure his own followed suit.

Guess that's my cue.

Leary got up from his chair, walked closer to where she was sitting, and got down on one knee. He raised the engagement ring. The diamond caught the light from the restaurant's chandeliers and sparkled.

"So we're going to do this the old-fashioned way this time?" Jessie said.

"Seems a little more romantic than doing it in between being tortured and running for our lives."

"Little bit."

The other diners in the restaurant took notice, and the murmur of conversation around them died. Waitstaff stopped in their movements to watch. Leary felt as if a spotlight had been aimed at him. He tried to ignore the attention. He reminded himself that only one person in this restaurant mattered right now. Maybe two, if you considered his future father-in-law helpfully loitering near the men's room door.

"Will you marry me, Jessie?" He lifted the ring to her.

"Yes, Mark. Nothing would make me happier."

Leary slid the ring onto her finger. His whole body trembled with excitement and happiness, a visceral, physical reaction he could not control, and didn't really want to—in fact, he wouldn't mind if the feeling lasted forever.

Jessie seemed filled with emotion as well, her smile as wide as he'd ever seen it. She wasn't looking at the beautiful diamond on her finger, though. She was looking into his eyes.

A round of applause thundered around them. Diners rose

from their chairs to clap, whistle, and tap their silverware against wine glasses.

Leary felt instant embarrassment, but not enough embarrassment to stop him from doing what felt natural. He rose to Jessie's height, pressed his lips against hers, and they kissed.

When they were back in their seats, Jessie's father returned. He showed Leary and Jessie a picture on the screen of his phone.

"You took that from inside the bathroom?" Jessie said with a wry smile.

"Ha ha. You think I'd miss my only daughter's marriage proposal?" Her father laughed. He gave Leary another affectionate pat on the shoulder. "You did great, by the way. Very chivalrous and romantic. You're a natural at this." He seemed to think about his own words for a second, and then added, "But don't think you're ever doing it again. This is a one-time deal."

"I'm in this for life, Mr. Black. Don't worry about that."

"I'm not worried at all," he said. "And call me Dad"

After dinner, Jessie and Leary walked back to their apartment holding hands. It was more of a public display of affection than they normally engaged in, but neither could resist. "I guess we'll have to tell everyone at work," Jessie said. Leary heard the note of nervousness in her voice.

"I don't think anyone's going to be too surprised."

She gave him a sidelong glance and bumped her hip against his as they walked. "Probably not."

"But just in case," Leary said, "maybe we should take tomorrow off. Spend it at home. In bed."

Her smile widened. "I think that's a very prudent idea."

46

JESSIE AND LEARY visited Kelly Lee's office about a week later. The Rowlands were there, as was Noah Snyder, who was filling a rocks glass with Scotch. Cheyenne was there, too, looking happy to be back at work, although still wary of Snyder.

"Anyone want a drink?" The silver haired lawyer smiled graciously, as if he were welcoming all of them to *his* office. "How about you, Leary? Jessie, you want another glass of my good stuff?"

Leary accepted a glass, but Jessie declined. Her focus was on Kelly, who seemed to be recovering reasonably well from her ordeal. Her body still bore the evidence of what she'd endured, and she would walk with a limp for the rest of her life, but the distant, shell-shocked expression she'd worn during her rescue had been replaced with the bright, intelligent look Jessie remembered from law school.

Kelly was working again. The class action suit was moving forward, and Jessie's understanding was that the case was progressing well. Kelly relied on Snyder to be the face of the team in court while she recovered. Kelly believed—probably correctly—that her physical condition would distract the jury.

But knowing Snyder as she did, Jessie assumed Kelly was doing all of the heavy lifting behind the scenes. Nevertheless, the two seemed to get along and make a good legal team.

The Rowlands, while not exactly happy, seemed to be in better spirits than the last few times Jessie had met with them. The progress they were making in their case against Boffo Products Corporation seemed to be having a healing effect on them, and they made no effort to hide their satisfaction about the mess of civil and criminal suits in which Douglas Shaw was currently embroiled. Jessie supposed no courtroom victory could ever heal the wound of a lost child, but she could see that it was helping. Maybe that was enough.

The door opened behind them, and Jessie and Leary turned. A large man burst into Kelly's office. He wore a bulky, ill-fitting suit, under which Jessie thought she recognized the bump of a concealed weapon. Leary stepped protectively in front of her.

"Get to cover," he said. The words came out quietly, through gritted teeth.

"You know this guy?"

"Shaw's personal thug. Met him at Boffo."

"This is a private office," Graham said. She had her gun in her hands. "Leave now."

The man didn't leave. He had the steely gaze and grim expression of a hardened criminal. Jessie's body went tense. She mentally braced herself for a firefight.

"I'm not going to ask twice," Graham said.

The tension in the room was abruptly broken by a laugh. It was Snyder, wearing a huge and very amused smile.

"Easy, supercop. Troy is a friend."

"He's no friend," Leary said. "He's one of Douglas Shaw's henchmen. A bodyguard or something. Trust me, we encountered this goon at Boffo's headquarters."

Snyder laughed. "This *goon*, as you call him, is the linchpin of our case. Jessie Black, Mark Leary, meet Troy Fowler. You remember when Kelly told you she had a mole inside Boffo who was helping her? Troy's the mole. When Kelly was thought dead, he stopped communicating. Can't really blame him. But now that Kelly's back, Troy is back, too, along with all his wonderful, juicy, incriminating witness testimony."

Leary turned to Kelly. His face looked incredulous.

Kelly nodded. "It's true."

Troy approached Leary and extended a hand. "Sorry I couldn't tell you. With Kelly gone, I didn't know who to trust."

Leary shook the man's hand. Graham put away her gun and did the same.

"No apology necessary," Graham said. "Thank you for doing the right thing."

Jessie felt a touch on her arm and turned to see Kelly looking at her with an uncertain expression. "Can we talk? In private?"

"Of course," Jessie said.

When they were alone in another room, Jessie said, "How are you holding up?"

Kelly's shoulders sagged, but then she seemed to rally. "I'm doing okay. I feel like I'm working through it. Sometimes, I still wake up in a cold sweat from nightmares, and sometimes I find my mind wandering during the day, or just, like, shutting itself off. But slowly, I'm becoming the old me again. I can feel it."

"Good," Jessie said.

"What about you?"

Jessie thought about it. She had a lot to be thankful for. She was engaged to the man she loved. The Rowlands' trial was back on track. Ray Briscoe was in custody—arrested by Lorena Torres —and facing murder charges now that the real identity of the body in Kelly's car had been formally established as that of the missing councilwoman. But Jessie still had sleepless nights. She would often lie awake thinking of what could have happened to her in Briscoe's torture room, and of what actually *had* happened. Sometimes she would remember, too vividly, the sensation of driving the scalpel into Briscoe's chest.

"I guess I'm working through it, too," she said.

"I never really thanked you," Kelly said. "I want to do that now. From what I've heard, you were the only person who didn't give up on me. You didn't believe the car accident was what it appeared. I owe you my life."

"You're welcome. But you don't owe me anything."

Kelly's gaze wandered to her feet. "Are we friends, Jessie? Ever since you got me out of that hellhole, you've seemed.... I don't know. Cold."

Jessie looked away. Had her feelings been so obvious? "It's nothing."

"Please, Jessie. If something's on your mind, just tell me."

Jessie took a breath and met the woman's gaze. "Emily Graham."

"The cop who helped rescue me?"

"The cop you brought a misconduct claim against years ago. A claim that was bogus and could have—maybe did—hurt her career."

Kelly took a step back. Her face changed as she seemed to remember. "I thought the name sounded familiar. Look, Jessie, if my client's claim wasn't true, I didn't know that. I—"

"It's not a one-time occurrence." Jessie felt anger rise within her like heat in her chest. She hesitated, not sure whether she should continue. Kelly was still recovering from a hugely traumatic event. Was this the right time for this discussion? But she continued because something inside her wouldn't let her remain silent. "It's a pattern, Kelly. Vicki Briscoe—"

At the sound of the woman's name, Kelly shuddered.

"The medical malpractice claim against Vicki Briscoe was false, too," Jessie said. "Leary talked to your client. We know you fabricated the lack of informed consent. You manipulated the facts to extort the hospital's insurance company, and in the process, Vicki Briscoe lost her job and her medical license. Her whole career."

"I think I've been punished enough for that."

Jessie didn't respond. Whether Briscoe's revenge absolved Kelly wasn't Jessie's call to make. She crossed her arms over her chest.

"The Rowlands' case is real. And from now on, cases like theirs are the only ones I intend to take. I'm done with the legal games."

"I hope that's true, Kelly."

"It is." Kelly shifted uncomfortably, almost shyly. "Do you think we could have lunch sometime?"

Jessie thought about it, then nodded. "Sure."

Kelly's face brightened. "I'd like that."

They returned to the main office, where Snyder was regaling his audience with a courtroom war story. Leary caught Jessie's eye from across the room. His expression asked if everything was okay. Jessie nodded, and walked over to join him.

Jessie took a deep breath of the elevator's stale but familiar air. It felt good to be back inside the Criminal Justice Center, where courtrooms buzzed with the routines and traditions of Pennsylvania criminal law and procedure. She touched the button for her floor. The elevator doors were about to close when Randal Barnes darted into the elevator.

"Morning, Jessie." The defense attorney smiled, catching his breath.

"Hi, Randal."

"I heard the big news. Congrats!"

Jessie touched her engagement ring. "Thanks."

"I'm sure you have a lot of planning to do, right? Picking a venue, a photographer, all that wedding stuff. An extra month should be a big help." He studied his reflection in the elevator doors, then ran his fingers through his hair until it stuck up in an unruly mess. He yanked the knot of his tie, making it loose and lopsided, then rubbed his eyes until they looked red.

"What are you doing?" Jessie said.

Barnes shrugged. "Gotta give Judge Bobblehead a decent

show, right? Woe is me, the overworked, overstressed, but valiant defense attorney, doing the best he can despite—"

"We're not postponing Alvarez's trial again," Jessie said, cutting him off.

"What?" Barnes reached down and stabbed the button to halt the elevator. The car rocked to a stop and a warning sound chimed. "What are you talking about?"

"You're going to withdraw your request for another continuance."

"Like hell I am. Tomas's mama still owes me three grand. Until she pays up, her baby stays in jail."

Barnes laughed. Jessie didn't.

"I'm serious, Randal. You're going to withdraw the motion."

His smile faltered. "Or what? You'll oppose it? Give me a break, Jessie. You'll lose. These motions are routinely granted."

"I don't think Judge Bobblehead, as you so respectfully call him, will agree once I fill him in on your shenanigans. Or when I introduce him to your client's mother." She watched Barnes's jaw open and his face drain of color, and tried not to enjoy the spectacle. "Then again, I doubt the Alvarez trial will be the first thing on your mind when you're dealing with the bar disciplinary committee."

"What's wrong with you? Why do you care about some gang-banger and his mother?"

"Maybe you should ask yourself why you don't. Why did you become a lawyer, anyway? Why don't you think about that?"

"You *are* serious," he said.

"We're going to trial."

She reached past him to the elevator's control panel and disengaged the emergency stop button. The elevator resumed its ascent.

When the doors opened, Barnes walked out, looking dazed.

Jessie followed him. She felt the beginning of a smile touch her face.

Yes, it was definitely good to be back.

THE END

Thank you for reading False Justice!

If you enjoyed the book, please post a review on Amazon and let everyone know. Your opinion will directly influence the success of the book. It doesn't need to be an in-depth report—just a few sentences helps a lot. If you could take a few minutes to help spread the word, I would greatly appreciate it.

—Larry A. Winters

BOOKS BY LARRY A. WINTERS

The Jessie Black Legal Thriller Series
Grave Testimony (limited time FREE offer)
Burnout
Informant
Deadly Evidence
Fatal Defense
False Justice

Also Featuring Jessie Black
Web of Lies

Other Books
Hardcore

Click here for the most up-to-date list of books.

http://www.larryawinters.com/books/

ABOUT THE AUTHOR

Larry A. Winters's stories feature a rogue's gallery of brilliant lawyers, avenging porn stars, determined cops, undercover FBI agents, and vicious bad guys of all sorts. When not writing, he can be found living a life of excitement. Not really, but he does know a good time when he sees one: reading a book by the fireplace on a cold evening, catching a rare movie night with his wife (when a friend or family member can be coerced into babysitting duty), smart TV dramas (and dumb TV comedies), vacations (those that involve reading on the beach, a lot of eating, and not a lot else), cardio on an elliptical trainer (generally beginning upon his return from said vacations, and quickly tapering off), video games (even though he stinks at them), and stockpiling gadgets (with a particular weakness for tablets and ereaders). He also has a healthy obsession with Star Wars.

Email: larry@larryawinters.com

Website and Blog: www.larryawinters.com

Facebook: www.facebook.com/AuthorLarryAWinters/

Twitter: @larryawinters

Grave Testimony, the exciting prequel to the bestselling Jessie Black Legal Thriller series, is FREE for a limited time. Click here to tell me where to send your FREE copy of Grave Testimony:

http://larryawinters.com/read-gt

You will also be included in my free email newsletter, where you'll learn more about me, my writing process, new releases, and special promotions. I promise not to spam you, and you can unsubscribe at any time.

—Larry A. Winters

Made in the USA
Las Vegas, NV
10 February 2022

43570079R00152